MW01224170

Cuba and Beyond . . .

The Journey

Diana Posada

Even though this book is based on an actual family's escape from Communist Cuba, it is partly a work of fiction. Some names, characters, places and incidents are the product of the author's imagination. In these cases, any resemblance to actual events, locales or persons, living or dead, is coincidental.

Dedication

To the love of my life, Felipe (Felipito) Joaquin Hildago Posada, my Cuban husband.

Acknowledgements

There are many people to be thanked for the existence of this book. My friends in The Falls at Eagle Crest, Redmond, Oregon, as well as members of its creative writing club who encouraged me to write this book. I am very grateful to Susie and Renney Senn, who spent many hours editing, providing sage advice and never-ending encouragement. My biggest thanks goes to my husband, Felipito, for sharing his life story with me. Of course, I also want to thank Felipito's mother, Clara, who, although she is deceased, told me many stories about Cuba before and after the Cuban repression that have found their way into this narrative.

Table of Contents

Chapter One—The Trip

I remember the 26th of May, 1960, vividly. I was tightly buckled in my seat and after a long wait in the hot, stuffy plane, the four engines were firing up on the Lockheed Super Constellation, fondly known as the "Connie." We had been sitting on the Havana airport tarmac a long time. My stomach was so full of butterflies there was not room for one more. The tension among the forty passengers was running high and hysteria hung in the air. Will the plane be cleared for takeoff or will all the passengers be pulled off the plane and imprisoned, or worse? I heard a woman behind me whispering the Lord's Prayer and somewhere a baby was crying. I closed my eyes and crossed myself, as she quietly finished her prayer.

I do not know how long we had been sitting there. Before I boarded the plane, a brusque, surly customs officer, while checking my passport, inspecting my suitcase, and performing a body search, snatched my watch and defiantly left me with an empty wallet. When he discovered my new United States permanent resident status "green card," he sneered and called over his superior, an army captain. Glaring at me, they both studied the card and my passport. I held my breath because I was sure they were going to destroy the card. The captain left with my documents and walked out of sight. I started to follow when I felt the customs officer's black wooden billy club pushing against my chest. The minutes slowly ticked by. Just when I was sure I would not be leaving, the captain reluctantly returned my documents and shoved me back in line almost knocking over a pregnant lady. After they finally finished, I was left with only the clothes on my back and one change of clean clothes wadded in my suitcase.

The plane slowly taxied to the runway. It appeared we were actually going to leave. Until the plane landed in Miami and I cleared American customs, I would not believe I had escaped Castro's cruel regime.

I closed my eyes and tears rolled down my cheeks. I would never see my homeland again. If I returned, it would be very dangerous for my friends and family. After Castro took power on New Year's Day, 1959, the government-controlled television station began broadcasting the killing of Cuban men and women by firing squad promptly at 6:00 every Saturday night. To instill more fear and demonstrate absolute authority, Raúl Castro and Che Guevara performed the final coup de gras by shooting each person in the head even though each was obviously already deceased. Fidel Castro and his henchmen declared them to be enemies of the new Cuba.

During one of Castro's two to three hour speeches, he glibly announced that all belongings, including homes, plantations, businesses, livestock, as well as their byproducts – eggs, cream, butter, and milk – were now considered the property of the Unitary Marxist-Leninist Communist Party. If an owner's chicken, cow, or pig were stolen or even died of old age, the owner was responsible for the loss and was required to reimburse the Party. My grandfather's cattle ranch, including the livestock, was confiscated and divided among the communists to farm collectively. The ranch quickly fell to ruin. The hospital and medical practice I was to inherit became government property, and my padre, Felipe, a surgeon, now received only a small salary.

There was another dictatorial edict that was quickly enacted and enforced by Che Guevara and his army squads. All citizens were required to turn in their firearms, including hunting rifles, shotguns, and even pellet guns. If you were found to be harboring a weapon, it was an automatic death sentence. My padre turned in his rifle and shotguns but instructed me to bury his pistol collection in oilcloth. We never dared to check their condition.

Neighborhood captains were posted to spy on people and keep order. If the captains did not like the way you looked at them, did not give them food, possessions, or money, you could face the firing squad. It was not unusual to hear screaming and crying in the middle of the night. Friends and neighbors, were forcefully hauled off, never to be seen again. It became a desperate time of fear and loss.

I am not sure what changed the Fidel Castro who had once declared he was a champion of the poor and young people. I was curious about his politics and beliefs. Now he was using our money to better only himself and his government higher ups. He quickly became worse than Batista, the president he worked so diligently to replace.

My madre, Clara, a psychologist, continuously begged me to leave. "Felipito, there is nothing left for you here. You will have no medical practice unless you pledge your life to the Communist Party."

Padre declared, "Son, this nonsense will soon pass. The Cuban people are strong and intelligent. They will soon come to their senses. You and I, together, will practice medicine and perform surgeries."

My parents constantly fought over whether I should leave or stay. Unfortunately, I could not complete my medical residency unless I pledged to become a communist. If I did this, I would not be allowed to live in the United States. The idealism of my youth for a new Cuba quickly deserted me. I took my mother's advice and made plans to leave. A close friend of the family, an American consul who lived in Cienfuegos, provided me with a green card (permanent resident status in the United States).

Once airborne for the thirty-minute flight to Miami, I began to wonder about my future. "What the hell am I doing? What am I going to do? I have never worked. I have neither money nor practical experience. I do have a medical degree after attending over sixteen years in the best and strictest private schools. I can only hope my Tia (aunt) Marta, who lives in Miami, will have a plan." I closed my eyes, my mind drifted, and I reminisced about my former idyllic life.

I was born in August 1937, and enjoyed a privileged life. My padre and madre were the darlings of high society in Cienfuegos. Cienfuegos was considered La Perla del Sur (The Pearl of the South) and is located on the southern coast of Cuba, approximately 160 miles from Havana. My father was thirty-six years old and my mother a mere nineteen when I was born. I was the apple of their eyes and was named Felipito (Felipe junior). My destiny was cast: I was to become a doctor and practice with my father. My education was planned from pre-school through college. I was enrolled in the Marista private boys schools that were administered and taught by highly educated Jesuit priests from Spain. My sister, Mirtila, born four years after me, attended private girls schools.

The family home was a grand, cream and white concrete and marble compound consisting of nine bedroom suites with bathrooms, sitting rooms, and living rooms. The estate had a beautiful courtyard and garden in the center. The house, constructed in 1862, was aptly named Casa de Los Leones (House of The Lions) and it was originally built to be a casino. However, by the 1870s, additional remodeling added living quarters and the property became the British Embassy. For many years the proud house was used to welcome dignitaries and host opulent banquets. The outside entrance portico perched at the top of a flight of stairs was supported by seven large pillars and guarded by two giant bronze lions sitting thirty feet apart. I never learned how the Hidalgo family (my grandparents) acquired the home.

The compound also included quarters for the servants, Maria, the cook, a cook's helper, three maids, and others as needed. Mirtila and I had a nanny named Nana until we started high school. We both loved Nana. She remained with the family, assisting in other areas. Upon marrying, my mother attended classes on how to manage a household. The staff both loved and respected her. My madre was full of life and enjoyed hosting parties. She was also active in Cienfuegos charities and societal activities.

I smiled and shook my head thinking about my padre. He was the exact opposite of my madre. He was a stoic man of few words and did not smile often. I believe my vivacious madre fascinated him. I often caught him looking at her in awe and other times in utter bewilderment.

When I was twelve, padre started my medical training. I observed him in surgery while standing on a box. By the time I turned fourteen, I was assisting him during surgeries. I also followed him on hospital rounds and met patients in his office. During patient consultations, I witnessed a different man. He compassionately listened to their maladies and kindly offered remedies. He told me it was very important to listen and study your patients as they shared their symptoms. You learn by listening and actually looking at your patient, not talking.

Even though my padre was a brilliant surgeon, he had absolutely no sense of direction. He was in constant contact with the city police department complaining that someone had stolen his car and demanding justice. The police dispatchers, familiar with padre's idiosyncrasy, patiently send an officer, who helped him search for his car. It was always found exactly where he had parked it. Unfortunately, I have the same characteristic and I am sure I inherited it from him.

Padre owned a forty-two-foot teak yacht that slept six, named "The Mirtila." The family would take the boat out in the bay so we could fish and swim. With no sense of direction, my padre never left sight of land. Even close to shore we caught grouper, sierra, red snapper, sea bass, yellowfin tuna, flounder, and more. We would either take them home to Maria for dinner or to the yacht club, where the French chef would prepare a wonderful feast. My favorite was the tasty white meat of the dorado. When we left the bay to fish in the Gulf of Mexico or the Bay of Pigs, padre always hired a skipper.

My padre's idea of the perfect evening after dinner was to smoke a fat Cuban cigar, drink fine French cognac, and read a medical journal or an historical novel. He played his black Steinway grand piano beautifully by ear. One of his favorite songs was Claire de Lune. He also enjoyed classical compositions by Chopin, Mozart, and Beethoven. However, my madre only allowed this a few days a week. She enjoyed dressing up in one of her many evening gowns and going out with my padre and friends to dine and dance in the supper clubs. Padre complained about going out but I think he secretly liked being seen with my madre. Her smile and laugh were infectious.

I also spent a great deal of time with my maternal grandparents, Juan Jose and Clara Hidalgo, at their sugarcane plantation named La Cristalina. I enjoyed the freedom of exploring the fields and outbuildings, stalking birds with my pellet gun, and helping my grandfather with his large plantation and equally large cattle ranch. My grandmother, like my madre, was joyous and doted on me.

My favorite time to visit La Cristalina was during harvest. This was always an exciting time with the dozens of employees swinging machetes to harvest the sugarcane. The cut sugarcane was loaded on ox carts and hauled to the train station where it was transported by rail car to coastal sugar mills. At the mills the cane was refined to brown sugar. The residual liquid from brown sugar, called black strap molasses, was stored in huge tanks. Tankers from the United States carried the thick liquid to be processed into molasses or liquor. Of course, this lucrative market with the United States quickly dried up after the communists came to power. The collective farms no longer produced the sugarcane efficiently and the US markets disappeared.

Many years before I was born, Juan Jose and a few wealthy friends decided Cienfuegos needed a private yacht club. A French neoclassical style building was built and the club became immediately successful. As an eighteen-year-old teenager, I spent many hours at the yacht club basking by the pool, eating meals provided by Mr. Mür, the French chef, and consuming exotic drinks. My favorite pastime, of course, was enjoying the scenery parading by. This was where I met my first love, Sharon. She was a blue-eyed, sixteen-year old, six-foot Canadian beauty. When she smiled at me and tossed her long golden hair, I was smitten. We spent the summer and winter together stealing kisses, giggling, and sharing love. I proposed, placed my grandmother Clara's exquisite two-carat diamond engagement ring on her finger, and we planned to elope. Unfortunately, her father, a civil engineer working on a hydroelectric project, did not approve of a 5'4" Cuban boy. When they realized they could not keep us apart, they quickly whisked her out of Cuba along with the ring. I later visited her in Montreal but she had already moved on with another beau. I was disappointed but I was soon busy with classes at the University of Havana.

Ahhhhh, Havana. I spent four glorious years soaking in the sights and sounds of the nightclubs, admiring the gorgeous women, drinking and dancing until the wee hours of the morning. I also studied to earn my medical degree, as my madre, who was studying for her doctorate in psychology, was not far away and kept a diligent eye on me. She kept the leash tight and controlled me with a meager monthly allowance. However, my friends and I soon discovered that with a smile and a corny pick-up line, many women would buy us drinks, after which we spent the nights visiting and dancing.

As the Connie was preparing to land, I opened my eyes and I saw the city of Miami getting closer by the second. I was cautiously optimistic I was safe. I just needed to get off the plane and clear customs. I was so close!

The impersonal customs officer glanced at my Cuban passport, examined my green card intently, and, looking me in the eyes, welcomed me to the United States. Smiling, I rapidly walked down a long corridor and, at the end, there was my tia (aunt), standing with arms open wide and a big smile on her face. I still had a lump in my throat, but now the butterflies were flying in formation. Marta is my mother's younger sister. She had lived in Miami for the last fifteen years and was a new citizen of the United States. After she finished college in the United States, her padre, Juan Jose, purchased a travel agency for her to manage. As family members left Cuba, it was Marta's job to help everyone acclimate to Miami and the United States. I was the first. She immediately recognized that I was nervous. She told me to relax; we would make it work. Then she said something I will never forget, "Felipito, let's go home."

Chapter Two—Marta

My Tia Maria, "Marta" Soledad Hidalgo Gruner, was born in 1926, making her only eleven years older than me. She was tall at 5'7," with brown eyes and light brown hair. She was a pretty girl and grew into a sophisticated, slender woman. Tia was the youngest of three siblings, therefore the most pampered. Her parents, Juan Jose and Clara, were quite wealthy. The wealth originated from Juan Jose's grandfather, also Juan, who was a businessman originally from Andalusia, Spain. He immigrated to Cuba in the mid-1800s to invest and grow his fortune. He stayed and married Soledad Ferrera, also of Spanish descent. The family tree of my madre and my tia's mother's was unique. Their abuelo (grandfather), Frederick Gruner, a German diplomat temporarily assigned to Cuba, never left. He fell in love with the country and one Ana Domingo Botignat. Her family, originally from Spain and France, left New Orleans,

Louisiana after the 1803 Louisiana Purchase was completed. The legend passed to each generation was that being of French descent, they did not want to live under the rule of the "barbaric" United States. However, madre quietly debunked the legend. She whispered, "Felipe, do not believe the stories. They were told that if they colonized the area now called Cienfuegos, they would receive land grants."

Madre added, "The majority of the immigrants traveled from the United States, while others came from Bordeaux, France. They were led by Don Louis de Clouet and settled here in April 1819. This is why the architecture is neoclassical and many of the avenues have French names."

I asked her, "Why was the city named Cienfuegos?"

She answered, "There are actually two theories. One story my mother told me is the settlement was named after a handsome Cuban Captain General named Jose Cienfuegos. The second theory made more sense to me. When the families landed, there were no buildings and, they were glad to be off the ship and camped on the beach. After nightfall, another ship arrived with supplies and counted one hundred fires on the shore. Thus the new town was named Cienfuegos (one hundred fires).

I always liked the romantic and adventurous legend of Captain General Jose Cienfuegos fleeing the barbarians, but I believe madre was right - my relatives had been promised and received land grants.

My abuelo (grandfather) and Marta's father, Juan Jose, graduated with a civil engineering degree from Tulane University located in New Orleans Louisiana. After graduation he returned to the family businesses in Cuba. Eventually he managed and owned a 1,000-acre sugarcane plantation named La Cristalina and an equally large cattle ranch. He was also the superintendent of a molasses tank storage company in Cienfuegos. He appeared to be stern but was actually a jolly, fun-loving man with many friends.

My tia was a bright youngster who attended Catholic girls schools and excelled academically. She never enjoyed playing with dolls and dressing up, attending dances, or wearing frilly, feminine clothes. She wanted to play baseball, climb trees, and shoot air guns with the boys. Unfortunately, since she lived in a macho society, these activities were never acceptable for a girl. Her family recognized that she was different and that Cuban society would never accept her gracefully. When it was time for her secondary education, my abuelo and abuela (grandmother), her father and mother, enrolled my tia in a Catholic girls school in Miami, Florida. She continued her education and graduated from the University of Virginia with a bachelor of science degree in business.

When my tia returned home for summer breaks and holidays, each visit confirmed to my grandparents they had made the right decision sending Marta to live in the United States; her clothing became progressively different. She replaced frilly blouses and full skirts with plain tailored blouses, jackets, pencil skirts, and trousers. They did not appreciate her rebellious attitude or her clothing choices.

Abuela admonished, "You are not allowed to leave this house with those disgusting trousers. No nice Catholic girls in Cuba wear trousers." tia loudly retorted and threatened, "My trousers are the latest fashion. The next time you see me, I will be wearing my pedal pushers!" They may have been high fashion and my tia's choice but my grandparents never allowed "those trousers" to be worn out of the house. Even as a young boy, I remember the heated arguments between tia and my grandparents. These loud conversations were always directed towards her clothing and radical attitudes. In hopes of a future marriage and grandchildren, they constantly paired her with local young men. Unhappily, these relationships failed.

Every time tia returned, there were numerous whispered conversations regarding her lack of a beau. Family friends and relatives were always curious about her departure to the United States. After she graduated from college and remained in the United States, it was even more scandalous that she was still single. The gossip was relentless. Embarrassed and uncomfortable, my tia's visits to Cuba became more infrequent.

In the late 1940s, my grandfather frequently flew to Miami to check on tia and visit with American friends. He soon realized there were

11

investment opportunities in southern Florida. Before 1950, he sold La Cristalina and used the proceeds to purchase vacant land in southern Florida zoned for apartment buildings.

Behind my abuelo's back, many friends and relatives in Cuba scoffed and laughed at his purchases. At cocktail parties, it was normal to hear, "Whatever is Juan Jose doing?! I hope he is not losing his mind. I feel so sorry for Clara. She must be beside herself. First it was Marta and now crazy Juan Jose." You see, my abuelo's land was literally a swamp and miles from Miami. However, with a rapidly growing population, Miami quickly spread towards his property. Swamps were drained and roads built, which allowed the development of commercial and residential properties. When abuelo built his apartment buildings, they were quickly rented. His naysayers were soon envious.

After tia graduated from college, abuelo purchased a travel agency where she could work and, ultimately, manage and own it. For twelve years she worked hard and the agency became profitable, requiring her to hire more employees to carry the workload. She marketed to large and small corporations alike and was soon favored to provide their business travel arrangements. Tia flourished in the United States and became a naturalized citizen.

With her warm smile and welcoming brown eyes, tia made friends quickly. She went to supper clubs, nightclubs, and art galleries, meeting many different types of people. Her friendships gravitated toward same-sex couples. However, she remained single.

In early 1960 during his last visit to Miami, abuelo gave tia a new assignment. He declared, "Marta, this is my last visit to Miami. The Castro regime revoked my travel privileges and they are becoming more entrenched every day. They have already confiscated all our businesses, properties, and bank accounts. I need you to help us leave Cuba and transition everyone to new lives in Miami and the United States."

The Castro regime had not yet totally closed the border but citizens had to formally petition to leave, which took months. As the families were allowed to leave Cuba and escape to the United States, it was her job to help with their assimilation. She provided housing, money, and assisted with employment opportunities. It was quite an assignment for a young woman in her thirties. However, tia was resourceful and stepped up to the plate to meet her responsibilities.

At the time of the purchase of the travel agency, no one could have predicted the important role tia and her business would play for family members escaping from Cuba who needed transitioning into their new lives. Not only did the travel agency book the airline tickets for the flights from Havana to Miami, tia always met and greeted the families at the airport. Upon arrival, they were always excited, bewildered, scared, and crying. Tia reassured them with hugs and kisses and instilled them with confidence and hope for their new futures. She also settled them in the apartment building owned by abuelo until they found jobs and housing. The majority who immigrated quickly assimilated and most became American citizens. However, there were some who planned to return to their homes in Cuba after the Castro regime was overthrown. They died dreaming of the old Cuba.

After many discussions, it was decided that my parents, who both had jobs, would remain in Cuba until the last family members were out. When a Cuban petitioned to leave the country, they were labeled gusanos (worms). As worms, they immediately lost their jobs, were removed from their homes, and had their monies seized. Instead of leaving them to live on the streets, my parents welcomed them to their home and provided them with food and shelter. After one family emigrated, another family member would formally request permission to leave. This continued until 1966 when Castro finally realized the majority of the people leaving were the well-educated, upper middle-class professionals. He quickly closed the border tightly. This included "open" communications. The government opened and read all correspondence before it left or entered Cuba. Many times letters were not forwarded and thrown away. Telephone calls were now very expensive and heavily monitored.

Tia was responsible for assisting all the Posada and Hidalgo families. She also helped my grandparents, Juan Jose and Clara Soledad, who arrived a few months after me. Abuelo was very resourceful, astute, and had predicted the future. Before Castro had taken over Cuba, he was able to transfer a portion of his wealth to the United States, which was a blessing. This enabled him to help family members with monetary support while his apartment buildings provided housing. One-by-one each family fled Cuba. In all, eight families escaped. They ranged from just an individual, like me, up to families of six.

In 1963, tia hired a new, attractive employee named Alicia. Fresh from a divorce, Alicia, also of Cuban decent, had experience working as an airline ticket agent. With a petite, slender build, Alicia had dark brown eyes, blonde hair, and a quick smile and laugh. She soon became an important part of my tia's life in more ways than one. Tia soon realized why she dressed differently and was not physically attracted to her numerous male friends. The friendship with Alicia grew into something special and a romance blossomed. They soon moved in together to begin their lives as partners. Unfortunately, this relationship also included Alicia's handsome ex-husband, who was a dashing airline pilot. Between flights, he bunked in their guest room and enjoyed eating the Cuban food tia and Alicia prepared. He bragged with stories of parties and interludes with stewardesses and passengers. After two years, they became bored with his stories and tired of his mooching and presence. Over dinner one night, they informed him the guest room was to be converted to a home office and furthermore, this was to be his last night. He smiled and suggested the lanai couch. In unison, they both shook their heads and adamantly said, "No." That was the end of the ex-husband's intrusion. The room remained an office until the mid-80s when it became a guest room for friends and family.

Tia and Alicia always had a small white poodle. Each lucky poodle was perfumed, pampered, and very spoiled. It always wore rhinestone collars, bows in its hair and pranced with painted toenails. Each pampered pooch visited the dog spa weekly. With never a dog hair out of place, each little darling was spotless. When it returned from outside after doing its business, its bottom was always cleaned. It went to work every day with its mothers where it lounged on a special bed or chair.

The loving relationship between my tia and Alicia endured for over fifty years. With the advent of internet travel, they closed the travel agency in the late 1990s. They also halted their globe hopping and stuck to cruising the Caribbean aboard ships embarking from Miami.

My tia is now a feeble ninety-one and has dementia. Of course, Alicia, in her mid-eighties, tia's best friend, companion, and the love of her life, is taking care of her.

Chapter Three—Felipe

My padre (father), Dr. Felipe Gonzales Posada Acosta, was born in 1900 in a small village near Cienfuegos. His father, Felipe Acosta, was an attorney and later a judge in Havana. When padre was a young boy, his madre (mother), Mirtila Posada, passed away. Obviously, she was a special person in his life as he named his daughter and yachts after her. Sadly, I never met my abuela (grandmother) and did not have a relationship with my abuelo (grandfather). He acquired his judgeship before I was born and I remember seeing him only infrequently. Padre had two younger sisters, Mirtila and Nana. Mirtila married a newspaper editor and lived in Havana. Nana, the youngest and my favorite, married Raphael, a civil engineer. They lived in Cienfuegos except when Raphael worked several years in Madrid, Spain.

Cuba and Beyond…The Journey

When I sat on her lap, Nana shared exciting stories about their adventures in Spain. I was mesmerized by visions of the gypsy flamenco dancers clicking castanets, stomping their feet, and twirling heavy skirts in tempo with the singers and guitars. Raphael and Nana's glorious meals started late at night and finished at 2:00 am. The handsome bullfighters wore colorful and sparkling clothes when they paraded and bowed to the cheers of the crowds as large black bulls circled. I decided that someday I would visit Spain.

Then one night I questioned my decision when I overheard Nana and Raphael telling my padre and madre about the horrors they had experienced in Madrid from 1936 to 1939 during Spain's Civil War. They were trapped and were not allowed to leave. All seaports, train stations, and borders were closed. According to the national newspaper, ABC, if they were caught trying to leave, they would be immediately executed by a firing squad. Out of sight, I shivered but continued to listen while trying not to breathe too loudly. During that period, Nana and Raphael were always hungry and lived in fear. I had always wondered why they were so thin; now I had my answer.

Nana said that when they ventured to the markets they never made eye contact with anyone on the streets. You never knew if they were a friend, an enemy, a Nationalist, or a Spanish Second Republican (pro Franco).

Both sides committed atrocities in each other's captured territories. Nana described a visit she had planned to the neighborhood butcher shop early one morning in hopes of purchasing a scrap of meat for soup. As she approached the shop, Nana heard screaming and saw people running away. In the shop window was a uniformed Republican officer hanging on a meat hook. When I overheard this, I gasped loudly. Discovered, I was immediately put to bed and admonished to never eavesdrop on adult conversations again.

As Nana sobbed, I heard my padre reassure her, "Do not worry, Nana, you and Raphael are safe. The Cuban people would never allow such barbaric acts." With my padre's prophetic words, I was able to sleep but I did dream about the man hanging in the butcher shop.

My padre, Dr. Posada, was a handsome, complex man with serious brown eyes and wavy dark brown hair. Even though he stood at only 5'8," I always thought of him as much taller. I remember he worked long hours at the hospital and private practice. His medical specialties were internal medicine and surgery. His practice included treating both the poor and the elite of Cienfuegos. He owned the local hospital with two other physicians, Dr. Rafael Diaz, a radiologist, and Dr. Roberto Hernandez, a urologist. The small hospital had twenty beds, four surgical suites, and an open room with several beds that served as what we would now call an emergency room. At late hours several nights every week, the home telephone would ring loudly and my padre would be off to the hospital.

Padre was a cultured man with expensive tastes. He loved a fine French cognac and a fat Cuban cigar. His closet was full of custom-made suits and shirts. He frequented an exclusive men's club called Liceo; located only one block from our house, it was definitely convenient for padre to visit. Women were not allowed unless the club held dinner dances. He felt comfortable and enjoyed conversing with the members. It was here that padre actually relaxed among his peers.

He and his sisters had been raised in a strict household with nannies and servants, where his father was the disciplinarian. Even as a small child and into adulthood, he wore only suits. I remember him rarely wearing the guayabera Cuban shirt with slacks, and I never saw him in shorts. The casual clothes only appeared when he went fishing, dove hunting, or visited the ranch and plantation. These activities were infrequent as he was always making rounds at the hospital or seeing patients in his office.

Medicine was his first love, but he also loved classical music. He was a very talented and accomplished pianist. Since he could not read music, he played by ear. With his eyes closed, he listened over and over to a particular song playing on the phonograph. Once he learned the tune, he hummed it as he moved his fingers slowly over the keys of his black grand piano. I was always amazed by how quickly he learned a song and loved watching his fingers speed over the ivory keys. I remember him playing classical favorites by Mozart, Chopin, Beethoven, and Debussy. My favorites he played were Moonlight Sonata and Clair de Lune. As he played, his eyes and face softened with a dreamy, far away expression; it was obvious he had become an extension of the piano and a part of the music.

At thirty-four years of age, my padre decided to join the exclusive Cienfuegos Yacht Club, so he contacted Juan Jose Hidalgo, my grandfather (abuelo), one of the founding members. In order for padre to meet more members, abuelo invited him to a formal dinner dance. Standing in his tuxedo, padre was smoking a cigar, drinking a single malt scotch, and conversing with abuelo when he spied an elegant young woman with coifed brown hair, dressed in a long, form-fitting, emerald green, satin evening gown. My madre was standing on the terrace laughing and visiting with friends. With the moonlight shining on her and the Cienfuegos bay, the setting resembled a scene from a romantic movie. "Juan Jose," my padre asked, "who is that divine young woman? I have never seen her before."

My abuelo answered with a smile, "Who? Oh, her. The young woman you are pointing at is my daughter, Clara."

Padre stammered, "I, I, I do not know what to say. She is very beautiful!"

Laughing, abuelo said, "She certainly is. She is only seventeen and is on spring break from the Sisters of Apostolic Girls School."

Padre said, "Oh, she is very young."

Puzzled and looking at him intently, abuelo answered, "Yes, she is young at heart, but she is mature for her age."

Hopefully, padre asked, "Could you introduce us? I would like to hear her voice…her smile and laughter are infectious. I cannot think of the words to describe them."

Smiling, abuelo replied, "Of course."

During the introduction, my suave padre, instead of shaking my madre's gloved hand, placed her hand to his lips and kissed it. As padre was holding my madre's hand, he continued smiling and looked at her face delving into her eyes. She returned his smile and demurely offered him her left hand to kiss also. Delighted, he did.

Padre smiled and asked her, "May I have this dance?"

Madre, holding up a small booklet, answered hesitantly, "Dr. Posada, I do not have your name entered on my dance card. I am supposed to dance with Gonzalo. However, I do not see him."

Before madre could change her mind or Gonzalo appeared, padre pulled her onto the dance floor. A Cuban song called Amapola (The Poppy) was playing. Since he did not like to dance, he was definitely not a good dancer. So, with great difficulty he attempted to glide madre smoothly over the dance floor while at the same time, with even greater difficulty, trying to think of something clever to say. He yearned to impress my beautiful young madre with an intelligent conversation.

He blurted out, "When do you return to school?"

Puzzled, madre glanced at his face and answered shyly, "Next week I return for my last semester before graduation."

"Miss Hidalgo, I would like to see you again. Will you join me for dinner tomorrow night?" he asked quickly with anticipation.

Blushing, she answered, "Dr. Posada, I cannot. We are leaving Cienfuegos tomorrow and going to our ranch in the mountains. Plus, I am not allowed to have dinner with you or anyone without papa's permission."

Taken aback and attempting to look confident as his mind raced for an appropriate answer, he stammered, "I-I apologize for being so forward."

Smiling coyly, and while looking deeply into his eyes, she said, "Dr. Posada, you are forgiven."

At this point, Gonzalo impatiently tapped him on the shoulder and declared, "I believe this is MY dance." Reluctantly, my padre acquiesced.

After the song finished, Gonzalo escorted madre back to her girlfriends, who had been watching the exchanges. Excitedly, they grabbed her and pulled her outside to the terrace where they quizzed her about her conversation with my padre, the most eligible bachelor in Cienfuegos. They demanded to hear every word that was said.

Madre giggled and said, "I cannot remember! I am so lightheaded, but I think he likes me."

Padre did indeed speak to my abuelo about seeing madre. Abuelo agreed to let him take her to dinner with a chaperone, but any additional dates would be her decision and, of course, always with a chaperone. Later, abuelo shared the conversation with madre. She nodded and smiled, trying to curb her excitement.

When madre returned from the ranch, there was a large fragrant bouquet of flor de mariposa (white ginger, also known as the butterfly jasmine flower) waiting. She found an envelope in the bouquet and opened it. Madre was not surprised to see they were from my padre. He was requesting to have dinner that evening and would pick her up promptly at 8:00. An unlikely romance between my older padre and my schoolgirl madre quickly ensued. A man of few words, he was puzzled by how much he looked forward to talking to madre about medicine and answering her questions. He also liked learning about her experiences at school and at the country properties my abuelo owned. He was not a romantic man and pondered how he would propose marriage. When he asked his colleagues how they proposed to their wives, they were astounded and of no help. He decided to ask a nurse he knew. She smiled and gave him a few ideas.

He bought a two-carat, marquise cut diamond engagement ring and called abuelo. Padre asked, "Juan Jose, can you meet tonight at Liceo? I need to talk to you." Abuelo agreed.

As abuelo and padre sat in white rocking chairs on the veranda, abuelo noticed padre was nervous and not sipping his first cognac. Finally, abuelo told padre, "I know what you want to ask me. The answer is yes."

Bewildered, padre stammered, "How do you know?"

Abuelo answered, "The way you and Clara look at each other. She constantly talks about you. Obviously you are both in love."

Diana Posada

Padre asked madre to accompany him to the yacht club. He secretly requested the orchestra to play Amapola. While they danced, he took the ring from his pocket and asked her to marry him. With tears in her eyes, madre answered, "Oh, Felipe, I would be delighted to be your wife!"

Not long after she graduated from school with honors, she turned eighteen and married Cienfuegos's most eligible bachelor, Dr. Felipe Posada Acosta, my padre. He was seventeen years older than her. However, her beauty, intelligence, and laughing eyes had captured his heart. Their weeklong honeymoon was spent at the South Beach Miami Florida Flamingo Hotel in the opulent honeymoon suite. My parents spent the week walking the beach hand-in-hand and eating romantic candle lit dinners, and, of course, without a chaperone. They also spent time in the casino and discovered neither one liked to gamble. I was born less than a year later; another male had captured my mother's heart. Padre was pleased to have a son destined to follow in his footsteps. Four years later, my sister, Mirtila, was born. It did not take her long to be daddy's girl.

When padre was home for dinner, we always dressed formally. I wore a suit and tie and madre and Mirtila were attired in nice dresses. The dinners were somber affairs, and, as children, we were to be seen and not heard. I never spoke unless I was asked a question, and I always provided a brief answer. The questions were invariably directed at school activities and academic subjects - especially math and sciences, grades, and the teachers. We were required to eat all the food prepared by the cook and placed on our plates by the maid. However, madre made sure the cook served only dishes that my sister and I liked in child-size portions.

I enjoyed visiting the kitchen. The Cuban cook madre hired, Maria, was a wonderful, plump, older woman with wild, curly gray hair that she tried to tame in a bun. She loved children. Always smiling, Maria would pull up a chair or sit me on the counter, explain the dishes she was preparing, and tell me about her grandchildren. There were always treats for me to nibble. I still remember with great fondness the smells and noises of the kitchen and how my love of cooking was born from watching Maria and

22

her staff prepare our meals. I do not believe padre ever visited the kitchen or talked to the household staff.

Communicating with women and children was difficult for padre. He struggled to find common ground for discussions. Looking back, I remember he was puzzled and perplexed about how to be a part of and function with his family. Basically, it was madre's job to run the household and raise the children. My padre was more comfortable with his peers; he was a man's man. As a child, my job was to behave and perform well in school. It never occurred to me not to have excellent grades.

Padre was a generous man. When family members found themselves in need of help, he was always there to provide financial or medical assistance. One particular family member, Padre's nephew, Pepito, did not like to work but was always coming up with get-rich-quick schemes that, more times than not, bordered on lawlessness. In Mexico, Pepito blindly and stupidly stepped over the line with one of his schemes and ended up in a filthy local jail. My padre traveled to Mexico and, to everyone's surprise and my Aunt Mirtila's relief, came home with Pepito. Padre never spoke of what he did to bring Pepito home. When I asked madre, all she did was rub her fingers together indicating money.

When families were leaving and immigrating to the United States under Castro's regime, he always helped them financially. Once they declared their intentions, Castro's government would immediately freeze their bank accounts and terminate their employment. Usually, they ended up penniless and had to wait months to be granted permission to leave.

During the revolution and after Castro came to power, padre truly believed that the Cuban people would come to their senses and overthrow this new, nonsense government. Throughout history, he did not realize that this type of totalitarian communism had never been successfully overthrown. His opinion was shared with only madre and me. With the presence of neighborhood captains and their spies, he never voiced his political opinions outside our home. Those who complained about the government or Castro disappeared, never to return, or they were openly executed by a firing squad. Padre started to doubt his convictions about how tenuous the new regime was when his hospital and medical practice were seized and declared to be owned by the government; he became a salaried employee. Unknown to all of us, he started stashing cash throughout the house. He knew it was only a matter of time before the bank accounts would be stolen. He never removed large sums from the banks, just a few bank notes here and there. He was right; ultimately, all the money my parents had saved was confiscated. Their accounts went from being robust to zero. They now had barely enough to make ends meet. Gone were the lavish parties, dances, and dinners out. The staff was let go and my mother and sister started cooking and cleaning the house.

When I was planning to leave for the United States, padre insisted I stay and practice medicine with him. I knew it was his dream that he and I would perform surgeries together, have our own patient loads, and confer on complicated surgeries and ailments. Medicine was the one subject about which he and I had long and involved conversations. When I left Cuba for the United States, he was well aware that we might never see each other again. Both our futures at this point in time, May 26, 1960, were unknown. The day I left was the only time I ever saw him become emotional. When padre and madre drove me to the Havana airport and walked me to the entrance, I saw tears in his eyes. He quickly brushed them away, hugged me, abruptly turned, and, with shoulders slumped, walked to the car and waited for my madre.

Cuba and Beyond...The Journey

Chapter Four—Clara

My madre, Clara, was a special woman. This opinion is not due to her being my mother. With a quick, radiant smile and laugh, and sparkling brown eyes, she was resourceful, intelligent, fun, loved life, and embraced challenges. These attributes greatly assisted Clara throughout her life. Madre, the oldest of three children, was born in 1918 to Juan Jose and Clara Hidalgo. Her life was planned and started with a comprehensive education in Catholic girls schools. When madre completed her education, she would have a doctorate in psychology. As a girl and young woman, she lived a very protected life and when leaving home was always accompanied by an adult. She was expected to study and obtain high grades in school, learn how to run a multi-faceted household, cook, sew, play bridge, swim, etc. She was doted on and spoiled by her parents, especially her father; Juan Jose adored her.

Cuba and Beyond...The Journey

During my childhood I observed that my parent's relationship, for the most part, was quiet, respectful, and reserved, mixed with loud explosions and tears. My madre was a force to be reckoned with. To this day, I believe my padre never completely comprehended what he had married. After the lavish wedding and honeymoon in Miami, madre quickly discovered freedoms she had not been allowed as a single woman. She did as she pleased, was not reserved, and was definitely not obedient.

When my padre was not home, the atmosphere was fun, filled with laughter, and the servants smiled. My sister and I were allowed to run loudly through the house playing games and chasing each other. Many times, madre participated in our antics and other times she read to us animatedly. When Padre was home, the atmosphere was formal and quiet. In this case, madre was respectful, as she understood he worked long, hard hours.

Once a week, madre hosted card parties. The bridge ladies spent more time gossiping than dealing cards. My sister and I used to hide and eavesdrop on their conversations. It was difficult not to giggle. If we did, a severe scolding ensued with a quick march to our rooms. No matter, we tiptoed to the kitchen where the cook always gave us treats.

At least two times each week, Madre and her friends dressed in fashionable bathing suits, and, with children in tow, went to the yacht club. The ladies' favorite suit was the new two-piece, either in floral or striped patterns. My madre's choice was a maroon-striped version. While the children swam, played, and fought in the large pool, the ladies, decked out in large straw hats dyed to match their suits and sunglasses, reclined on the chaise lounges, visited, and drank large tropical drinks.

Culture was very important to my madre. She loved music, ballet, and opera, plus the modern Cuban and American singers. She worked hard to instill these same values in my sister and me. She was successful with my sister but not so much with me. She had always wanted me to be able to impress her friends and my padre with my fingers skillfully playing beautiful piano melodies. Unfortunately for madre, this was never to be. I absolutely hated piano lessons and practicing was one continuous battle after another. I exasperated many cranky tutors who all explained to a protesting madre, "Your son has no musical talent!" She reluctantly acquiesced. My sister was a better pianist and took lessons for seven years. However, Mirtila's joy and forte was ballet. To me, the ballet recitals I was forced to attend were very dull and boring. I developed the dubious skill of fidgeting. Today, children no longer fidget. Instead, they are considered hyperactive and are given medication for attention deficit disorder. If they had had Ritalin in the 1940s, I would have been a star candidate. On more than one occasion, I was shushed and had angry fingers shaken at me. This happened whenever I was expected to sit quietly for more than five minutes. Madre absolutely loved going out to dinner and dancing. She made sure she and padre were out at least once a week with friends or family. My padre was not a willing participant, but he knew that if he did not go, an explosion would ensue. Whenever madre was dressing for an evening out, she always hummed her favorite songs.

In August 1939, my padre arrived home very proud and waved a packet of papers in the air, shouting, "Clara, Clara, we are going to the World's Fair in New York City! I have all the tickets and have made the hotel reservations. We leave in two days and will stay for two weeks."

Shocked, my madre quickly retorted, "Felipe, we cannot go. I have Felipito's second birthday party planned. It is to be held in only four days. All the guests have RSVP'd and the preparations have started. You need to rebook for another time."

"But Clara, I did this for you. For years you have wanted to visit New York City. Besides, all the buildings at the fair have electrification! The fair is about how machines will affect our futures, like the new picture box called television. They even have a newly invented dishwasher! There are exhibits from different countries throughout the world. You will love it!"

Dejected, padre left for the World's Fair alone. My madre stayed behind for my birthday party and entertained the guests. Padre's journey from Cuba to New York City was to take two days, and the return two more days, leaving ten days to tour New York City and the Fair. However, within six days, padre returned. He announced that he had seen everything he needed to see. My madre nodded knowing that even if she had gone, he would have probably demanded to return home early.

When I was four years old, my madre was horrified to realize that I was not as tall as her friends' sons. I returned from pre-school one day and heard my madre and abuela (grandmother) whispering. Madre observed worriedly, "Felipito is small for his age, and he is definitely shorter than other four-year olds, even the girls."

Abuela replied, "Clara, he is small and shorter but remember, you may be 5'8" and your husband 5'9," but look at me; I am barely 5' tall! Maybe he is short because of me."

"I know you are short but he has two tall parents," my madre pointed out excitedly. "There has to be something wrong with him. Surely there are medications available to make him grow!"

"Clara, I do not think there is anything that can stimulate growth. However, maybe he needs more vitamins. Maria Sanchez told me her granddaughter was very tiny and unhealthy. She said her abuela suggested that she give her a tablespoon of cod liver oil two times a day. The little girl, Rosa, became very active and gained weight. Maybe this would help Felipito grow."

My madre replied, "Madre, I certainly make sure my children have sufficient vitamins and eat healthy food. However, you may be right. The cod liver oil could be the answer. When Felipe comes home, I will talk to him. I am sure he will know what to do."

Unfortunately, my first dose of cod liver oil was administered before my padre returned from the hospital. It was very nasty stuff indeed!
Padre attempted in vain to explain, "Clara, Felipito is small and short. Your mother is correct. She is barely 5' tall. You are tall because your father is tall. Juancho and Marta are both shorter than you. Leave the boy alone. He may or may not grow."

Diana Posada

Madre was not pleased with my padre's answer. There were words and more words growing louder and more heated with each exchange. Finally, padre, out of frustration, threw his hands in the air and said, "Clara, since you have already made up your mind, I will make an appointment with my friend Fernando Martin, an endocrinologist in Havana. We will let him decide if he can help with Felipito's growth."

After Dr. Martin examined me, he visited with my padre and madre. He was well aware of madre's concern. He kindly told my parents, especially madre, "Felipito is going to be a short man. He will grow to a height of 5'5." Upon receiving the news, madre sobbed.

As soon as we returned home, the cod liver oil treatment, one tablespoon two times each day, continued for a miserable six months. She checked my height every week. I did not grow. One day the treatments quietly ceased. I was elated and decided against asking why.

In 1954, with only a nominal allowance, I moved to Havana to a boarding house with nine other University of Havana students. Madre also enrolled in the university to receive her doctorate in psychology. Since I was impressionable and naïve, she said she did not want me in Havana alone with all the casinos and bordellos. She found an apartment and commuted between Havana and Cienfuegos on weekends. Padre was not happy with the arrangement but allowed her to finish her own education while she kept an eye on me.

In 1957, University of Havana students listened daily to short wave radio station broadcasts from the revolutionary Fidel Castro. Castro and eighty-two guerillas had secretly arrived in Cuba from Mexico, on December 2, 1956, and were hiding in the Sierra Maestra Mountains. Castro and his campus recruiters used the broadcasts to build a multi-class fighting force to overthrow the Batista government. Impressionable young people and peasants were mesmerized and excited by these broadcasts. Day after day, every broadcast consistently delivered the same messages: Castro promised to help the poor and uneducated achieve better lives and to oust the greedy, evil dictator, Batista. He encouraged the citizens to join Castro's army; he needed everyone's help.

Madre witnessed the enthusiasm of pro-Castro students growing stronger every day. Some of my friends even started talking of joining the revolution while others participated in rabble rousing on campus. They were burning cars and effigies of Batista. Madre became alarmed. She did not want me involved and secretly understood what was coming. She also believed that if Castro came into power, I should speak English. The United States may be my new home. She insisted I return with her to Cienfuegos and my padre. Of course, I did as I was told. They made arrangements in conjunction with the university for me and three other students to travel to Georgia in the US for six months to learn English.

As young, handsome Cuban men, we were treated as celebrities and enjoyed the hospitality of the Georgia girls. When our English classes were completed, we were definitely sad to leave. We were all able to read, write, and speak English, albeit with heavy Spanish accents. We soon discovered that girls enjoyed our accents and, of course, we used them to our advantage. To this day, I still have a warm place in my heart for Georgia.

In June, 1959, my madre received her doctorate in clinical psychology. I graduated with a medical degree and wanted to immediately start my internship, but with the Castro uprisings increasing and becoming more violent, the program was suspended. When Castro overthrew the Batista government, I was able to enroll only if I formally declared my loyalty to the Communist Party. However, I was warned by the American Consulate located in Cienfuegos that if I signed this Communist oath my immigration to the United States would be impossible.

After listening to months of arguments between my parents, witnessing my homeland change for the worse, and watching my friends leave, I made my own decision. One night at dinner I announced, "Please stop arguing about my future. Both of your arguments make sense. However, I have decided to leave."

Quickly my madre made the arrangements for me to leave the country. This was another argument where my madre prevailed. For days, my madre and padre did not speak to each other. I had never seen my padre this angry with her. As I packed a few belongings to leave, the atmosphere at home was extremely tense.

The long drive to the airport was somber. The goodbyes at the airport with madre and padre were painful. During the farewell hugs and kisses and last minute instructions, madre remained stoic until I picked up my suitcase and turned to walk away. As I stepped through the airport doors, I can still remember her sobs and her crying as she said, "Goodbye, Felipito, I will never see you again."

Chapter Five—Felipe and Clara—Bay of Pigs

At dawn on a Saturday in March 1961, my parents were awakened to shouting and loud pounding on their front door. Padre grabbed a dark maroon velvet robe, hastily slipped his arms into the sleeves and tied the silk belt. He opened the door to see Block Captain Jorge Elizondo and two soldiers he did not recognize. Jorge sternly demanded padre accompany them to the Cienfuegos Communist Headquarters.

"Jorge," Padre quietly asked, "may I change clothes?"

Captain Elizondo hesitated and retorted, "Yes, you may. We will wait in the parlor."

Padre hurried to the bedroom where my frightened madre met him. Padre put his finger to his lips and whispered in her ear, "Keep your voice very low. They are in the parlor." Madre nodded and tightly hugged him.

Padre continued whispering, "Clara, you have to be strong. Go about your normal business as if nothing has changed. Do not use the telephone. If I am not back by nightfall, gather a few belongings, money, slip out the

33

back, and go to Mirtila's house. Do not, and I repeat, do not leave before dark. I am sure the house is being watched." Bewildered, madre nodded.

My padre quickly dressed in his normal day-to-day attire, a dark blue suit, white starched shirt, and a matching dark blue and maroon tie. He checked the mirror and hoped he did not look nervous. The last thing he wanted was to appear scared. After my padre and madre tightly hugged one last time, padre briskly walked to the parlor to meet his fate.

As the front door closed, madre overheard padre ask Captain Elizondo about the captain's mother, who was one of his long-term patients. Feeling hopeless and lost, madre sat on the bed and tried to plan her day. She knew she had to keep busy, very busy. First, she forced herself to eat a simple breakfast of toast and a poached egg and then cleaned house. Since Castro had come to power and they had started to live on salaries, they had adapted to a different lifestyle. It was a sad day when she had to tell the household staff she could no longer afford to pay them. They all hugged and cried. Sadly, only Nana, the nanny, and Maria, the cook, had located positions in the homes of the new communist leaders. Madre wished she could have helped the others, but since my parents were assisting family members to leave Cuba, they were financially stretched.

At the open-air black market madre purchased dinner, consisting of a chicken, short grain rice, a red and a green pepper, two red tomatoes, garlic, onions, peas, a pineapple, and fresh crusty Cuban bread. She picked a couple of ripe avocadoes from their courtyard tree. Even though she had spent the week's food budget, she decided to cook padre's favorite meal, arroz con pollo (chicken with rice) and a pineapple-avocado salad. Walking the mile home from the market, she worried about my padre and, if necessary, the timeline of her escape. When drawing closer to home, madre smiled and greeted a few neighbors, who avoided eye contact, and offered a brusque, "buenas dias," as they scurried away. Madre was puzzled, and then rolled her eyes as it dawned on her, they knew! She wondered how, and then remembered the loud knocking and shouting.

Cuba and Beyond...The Journey

Upon entering the house, madre heard the white and gold telephone ringing. She debated on whether or not to answer. She followed my padre's instructions and ignored the annoying high-pitched rings. She changed her street clothes to a housedress, donned a ruffled yellow apron, and started dinner. The task of cooking helped to take her mind off Felipe.

The shadows lengthened and evening approached. With comforting kitchen aromas, she set the table. With a glass of Spanish red wine from her last bottle, she retired to the parlor, sat in a light blue easy chair and impatiently waited, crossing and uncrossing her legs. For her, time was at a standstill and she worried. Every few seconds, she nervously glanced at her watch. Just as she stood to walk to the kitchen and pour a second glass of wine, the front door opened. Startled, she peeked around the parlor door. She crossed herself and mentally thanked God; padre had safely arrived home. He looked very tired and grim.

Madre walked toward him and asked if he would like a scotch. He nodded and gave her a quick hug. She looked to him for answers but he volunteered nothing. They moved to the living room and he gulped his drink. She poured him a second. He finally spoke. He needed to take a shower to remove the smell of that dreadful place.

Over dinner, padre told madre about his long, horrible day. With a deep sigh, padre started by telling her that they took him to a windowless, stuffy room that smelled of urine, and left him alone for over ninety minutes. For the next two hours, Captain Elizondo and another officer rudely and loudly accused him of having no loyalty to Cuba and the Communist party. They repeatedly pounded the table and shouted in his face that he was a traitor and if he did not confess, he would be shot.

"Clara," Padre whispered, "Over and over I told them that I loved my homeland." My madre stood up and walked over to him and put her arms around him and gave him a hug saying, "Felipe, you are home and safe."

Padre, shaking his head added, "When I thought I was doomed, they left the room and returned a few minutes later. They were totally different!"

"It was as if we were comrades and good friends," he added. "I was shocked. Then they told me the real reason for my 'visit' to headquarters."

He explained to a floored madre that Castro's extensive spy network, with the help of the Russians, had uncovered a plot for an invasion by the United States, Cuban exiles, and local dissidents. He added that several other surgeons and nurses were being conscripted to serve as a front line medical corps for the Cuban military. He was to leave in two days to organize and set up a field hospital between Cayo Ramona and San Blas, not far from the Bahia de Cochinos (Bay of Pigs). He had no idea how long he would be gone. Padre ended by telling her to continue her normal routine and to not, and he repeated, not tell anyone, not even family members, the reason for his absence. Just explain that he was in Havana for meetings and training. Madre silently nodded her head in agreement and wondered if this mess would ever be over.

In two days, padre was picked up and escorted again by Captain Elizondo. He joined other medical corps members consisting of four surgeons, twelve nurses, and approximately one hundred support staff, including armed guards. They were loaded into trucks for the hundred-mile journey. The main highway was paved, but once they turned toward the bay, the dirt road was a washboard filled with potholes. The four-hour journey was tiring and padre was thankful when the jolting trip ended.

The soldiers quickly constructed tents for living quarters, a kitchen, and a dining area. Two doctors were quartered in each ten by twelve foot camouflaged canvas tent. The fifty-bed hospital consisted of five large fourteen by twenty foot tents for patients with varying degrees of injuries and recovery length. Since the camp was located near a large swamp, the cots were crowned with mosquito netting. Another four, identically sized tents were set up for surgeries. Over the next few days, padre and the other medical corps members organized their surgical theaters. Then they waited. They were not allowed to walk past the camp's perimeter and were watched continuously. Many played cards or read. Since padre didn't play cards, he read or walked around the camp. He was glad he had packed several books and grateful that madre had insisted he leave his normal attire at home, opting instead for more comfortable slacks and Cuban guayabera shirts. It was hot and the humidity was high.

During his camp wanderings, he pondered why the invasion was planned to take place in such a flat, inhospitable, swampy area and not closer to the mountains near Casilda and Trinidad. These mountains definitely would have provided more cover for the dissidents and invading forces. He shook his head, kept walking, and knew there would be many casualties.

April 17, 1961 arrived, and the invasion began. Padre's camp was awakened at midnight by the sounds of gunfire. Everyone was told to stay in their tents with no lanterns. The silence was deafening, only to be interrupted by brief squawks from the handheld radios crackling with updates. Before daybreak, the invasion forces started arriving on the beaches from ships anchored off shore. Almost immediately, the poorly trained exiles and guerillas clashed with Castro's government forces and militia. The fighting was fierce, but the exiles were outnumbered and doomed from the start. Communications were almost nonexistent for the insurgents as the radios were drenched during the landings. Unruly waves caused many to lose their weapons, ammunition, and equipment, and the transports that carried medical supplies sank. The fighters quickly ran out of ammunition.

Padre was correct, the area was flat and offered no concealment, and the invading forces were easily picked off. To make matters worse, the air and naval support the United States promised never materialized. The ships sat idle and frustrated crews were ordered to stand down. The only assistance they could offer was to bring aboard survivors who happened to make it back to the ships. With their hands tied, they could only watch the grim carnage through powerful binoculars and hope that there would be some survivors.

The CIA had not thoroughly researched the area and had refused to listen to the pleas of the dissidents. During numerous meetings, the dissidents repeatedly explained to CIA planners that the designated landing area would not work and they could be attacked from the shoreline. The worst happened and, of course, the CIA operatives were dumbstruck when Castro's militia attacked from the San Blas road and the shoreline from Cienfuegos. The untrained 5,000 Cuban citizen militia had traveled during the night concealed by darkness. The dissidents were surrounded in a pincer movement and quickly overrun.

Armed exiles also unsuccessfully tried to hold the main road but were quickly overwhelmed by battle-seasoned Cuban government forces personally trained and led by Che Guevara.

Four days later, on April 21st, it was over, and the sacrifice was felt by both the United States and Cuba. On the invaders' side, 128 Cubans died and 1,202 members of Brigade 2506, consisting of exiles, were captured. On the government's side, 176 Cuban armed forces died. The poorly trained Cuban militiamen, consisting mainly of peasant "volunteers" who were placed directly on the front lines, lost 4,000, with another 500 wounded. Che Guevara provided gleeful television and newspaper interviews proclaiming the superiority of the Cuban forces and how they easily defeated the traitors and the imperialistic, cowardly United States.

Padre and members of the medical corps worked non-stop, day and night, to care for the wounded. Their little hospital was soon full. Those who were "patched up" and needed additional surgeries or longer hospitalization were transported to hospitals located in Cienfuegos and other nearby towns. Padre was surprised when Che and his entourage showed up to visit the wounded. Padre noticed the smiles, congratulations, and handshakes did not begin until flashbulbs popped and cameras recorded the "humanitarian" Che during the propaganda tour.

One afternoon, during a much needed break, padre stepped out of the surgical theater and observed wounded men who were tossed roughly on the ground; some were even kicked and punched. The men moaned and many were crying. He was immediately drawn to help. After only two steps, padre was halted with a rifle pointing at his chest. The soldier angrily shouted, "You are not to help the traitors, only the heroes. You touch the traitors and I have orders to shoot you."

A week later, when padre returned home, madre greeted a different man. His shoulders sagged, his demeanor was that of a beaten dog, and his eyes had lost their sparkle. He looked at her, sighed, and said, "Clara, you were right to encourage Felipito to leave. This Communist regime is here to stay, as well as Cuba's loss of empathy and humanity."

From April to October 1961, my parents watched on television as hundreds of people were executed or imprisoned for a minimum of thirty years. In March 1962, the Brigade 2506 members stood trial for treason. My parents were not surprised when all were promptly pronounced guilty and sentenced to thirty years in prison. In April, sixty of the wounded or ill prisoners were released and returned to the United States. In December, they were even more surprised when the United States and Castro agreed to exchange all the Brigade prisoners for fifty-three million dollars in food and medicine. In addition, 1,000 of the brigade's family members were allowed to leave. For months, there were numerous speeches by Castro and Che Guevara bragging about their magnificent victory over the imperialistic United States. They reminded madre of prancing and crowing roosters who ruffled their feathers to impress the hens.

Padre finally agreed with my madre and they finalized plans to escape. However, they decided it was still important for them to continue helping all their family members escape and be the last to leave.

Diana Posada

Chapter Six—Felipito

"Felipito? Felipito?" tia Marta called. "Are you still lounging by my pool?" She had just returned from a long day working at her travel agency. I answered, "Yes, tia. What else would I be doing?" I was embarrassed but glad to have the company. It had been a long three weeks since I had left my homeland. I felt lost and was not sure what to do. I knew I needed to work but had no idea how to start the process.

Marta poured two glasses of Spanish temparillo wine, sliced a baguette from a local Cuban bakery, added cheddar cheese slices, and joined me by the pool. Over the last few days, I noticed her impatience growing. She thought of me as lacking initiative and ambition. However, today her attitude appeared different.

She explained, "This afternoon it hit me like a lightning bolt. Since you have never worked, you do not know how to start a job search. Felipito, I want you to join me at my office tomorrow. You and I will develop your résumé, and I will also coach you on how to approach and interview with prospective employers."

All morning she peppered me with job interview questions and typed my résumé. To make copies, Marta used three carbons stacked in between four crisp white sheets of paper. When she finally pulled the completed document from the gray Remington's rollers, I noticed she whispered a silent prayer.

She looked at me intently and stated, "Felipito, in order to land a job you need to lose your cocky attitude and that touch of arrogance written all over your face, walk, and body language.

Grimacing she added, "As an employer I know your job search it going to be an uphill battle. It is going to be a hard lesson but it is one you have to learn on your own."

Incredulous I answered, "Tia, don't worry I will have a wonderful job by tonight!"

Shaking her head in disbelief, Marta gave me a Miami city map, wrote down the bus route numbers—one to arrive downtown and another for the return trip—provided me with bus and lunch money, and sent me on my way.

In 1960, Miami's economy was booming due to tourism. With the renovation of a barely adequate airport into a modern international hub, tourists from South America and Europe began flocking to the area. The streets were congested, noisy, and could be dangerous. Dressed in a navy suit (my only suit), white starched shirt, and maroon tie, I wandered downtown Miami's crowded, busy, sweltering sidewalks. I was convinced that after entering the first place of business, I would be hired. I briskly walked into a car insurance office, and, with a heavy accent, asked to speak to the manager. As the blonde receptionist looked me up and down, she made a brief call and then quickly told me no. All afternoon, the only words I heard were emphatic "No's." When I finally boarded bus #120 to return home, I stood sandwiched between a smelly, heavyset man, and a tall brunette woman. My feet throbbed, and I was hot, tired, cranky, and disappointed.

When I walked into my tia's office, the look on my face said it all. Her prediction was correct. On the drive home, I told her about all the doors slammed in my face. Humoring me, Marta told me that tomorrow would be better. With my medical degree, she suggested I try the hospitals. One of my father's good friends, an internist, Dr. Vincente Fernandez, practiced at Mercy Hospital. With renewed hope, I planned to visit him first thing in the morning.

I boarded bus #150 near my tia's office carrying a city map and the bus numbers to Mercy Hospital and back. Once at the hospital, I waited impatiently for three boring hours, reading all the outdated Look and Life magazines, to see Dr. Fernandez. The waiting room was continuously full until noon. At last, Dr. Fernandez greeted me warmly and asked about my padre. I shared my journey from Cuba, leaving my homeland, and my parents' decision to stay and help others family members in their plight to leave.

I quickly added, "I need to work and I am not sure what I can do. What do you suggest?" Dr. Fernandez sadly shook his head and replied, "Felipito, I wish I could hire you but I cannot. For you to practice medicine, you need to return to school and complete your internship." Trying not to look too disappointed, I thanked him for his time and, deflated, returned to my tia's office. During the bus ride back, I seriously considered returning to Cuba. There was nothing here for me.

Finally, after another long embarrassing week, I entered Weizmann and Son's jewelry store. I asked to speak to the owner. I was surprised when I was ushered in to Avi Weizmann's office. For thirty long minutes I sat in a hard wooden chair as an unsmiling Mr. Weizmann asked questions regarding my background and education. Finally, I was told to show up promptly at eight the next morning to start my sales training. My salary was to be five dollars paid in cash per day.

Diana Posada

Showing up early for work and expecting to sell jewelry, I was dismayed when I was instructed to clean the bathrooms, including the toilets, morning and night, polish the silver, and keep the glass showcases spotless. I quickly realized the sales position was secondary. I served only as a translator and did not receive a commission. At the end of every day, I was given a five-dollar bill. I was bored and not happy with my employment but I had no choice.

While I polished the silver, my mind wandered to my carefree days in Cuba with my two best friends, Pedro and Aleandro. For years, every morning they stopped by my house and the three of us proceeded to roller skate the two miles to school. We dared not be late. Our first class, physics was taught by Father Julio Garcia, a Jesuit priest from Spain, and he was greatly feared. He appeared to be a round, jolly man, but he was a stern taskmaster. I smiled and concluded that Father Julio was an excellent teacher even though he often rewarded us with hours of homework or prayers in the school chapel. Of course, with no time constraint, the return home from school was often filled with mischief.

Sadly shaking my head, my educational path had prepared me to work in medicine with my padre but certainly did not apply to my current dilemma. Wistfully, I smiled as I recalled the luxurious Miami Fontainebleau Hotel I once frequented with my parents; it was now a lifetime away. I could not even afford a drink there, let alone to spend the night. I now understood that my decision to leave Cuba was easy compared to the consequences I now faced.

After two months of sheer boredom and daily humiliation, I arrived home to a smiling Marta. She finally had a plan, and what a plan it was! Excitedly, she shared a conversation she had had with a client. "Felipito, I spoke with Jorge Gomez regarding your plight. He suggested you contact an army recruiter. His cousin, Manolo, was able to finish his medical education in the Army. I have the address of the Army recruiting office. You need to go there tomorrow during your lunch break." With a huge smile on my face, I kissed my tia on the cheek and said, "Let's go out and celebrate!"

Cuba and Beyond...The Journey

Smiling, I briskly walked into the Army recruiting office and came face to face with an unsmiling recruiter. The soldier, Sergeant Richard Simonson, hid a smirk as he examined me, a short, cocky Cuban standing in front of his desk, and asked, "May I help you?" With a heavy accent, I answered, "Yes, I am here to enlist." The sergeant sighed and motioned me to sit. We spent the next hour discussing the Army and how to complete my education. I was also informed that by enlisting my road to citizenship would be much faster and easier.

When I left, I was both disappointed and excited. The armed forces no longer offered the programs for doctors to complete their education. I had only three choices if I wanted to enter the medical field, and I would be required to pass a rigorous written aptitude test. Of the three choices, I opted for the radiology technician program. I was not interested in nursing or being a laboratory technician. My test was scheduled for the following week. Once I passed the exam and received a letter from the Army assuring me that I was to attend radiology school, I would be sworn in. Of course, I aced the test and enlisted on August 25, 1960.

I completed my basic training at Fort Jackson, North Carolina. I was the oldest recruit in the group, but at least not the shortest. Harold Shaw from Louisville, Kentucky, was an inch shorter. In early April 1961, I was stationed at Brooke Army Medical Center, San Antonio, Texas to complete my radiology technician training. The 418-bed hospital built in 1937 was a part of Fort Sam Houston and had actually started as a humble dispensary in 1879. Between 1929 and 1933, under the direction of Brigadier General Roger Brooke, the first chest X-ray was employed and used as a diagnostic tool. To honor him and his discovery, the hospital was named after the general. During World War II, the hospital grew in size and reputation as a world-class care center. The more seriously wounded from the World War II battlefields came to Brooke. The numbers were so large that a 220-person barracks was converted to hospital patient wards. By the Korean War, the hospital treated causalities with short- and long-term care. During the early

1960s, the hospital had become a training center for many medical specialties, including veterinary medicine.

I sure did not miss polishing silver, and thoroughly enjoyed my return to the busy bustle of a hospital atmosphere. I was in awe of the medical center and beautiful park-like grounds surrounding it. My padre's hospital in Cienfuegos was smaller than the emergency department at Brooke General. During a lunch break on April 20, 1961, I picked up a discarded newspaper. I read and reread the headlines and stories regarding the Bay of Pigs. I was befuddled and became very worried about my friends and relatives in Cuba. I rushed to a telephone booth and used all my dimes and quarters to call tia Marta. She had no news other than what was in the newspapers and on the television.

After class, I wrote and mailed a letter to my parents and watched the news in a student lounge. I paced and walked the grounds. I sat on a park bench and wondered if I should try to call my parents. I knew I would probably not get through; my tia had tried unsuccessfully several times. Frustrated, I walked back to the barracks. I hated being in this impossible position. With a lump in my throat I stopped at the chapel and prayed I would receive an answer to my letter. It was my only hope.

I started hearing and reading about the Bay of Pigs' consequences for the United States and the news was not good. In fact, the news was horrible. Both the newspapers and television shared many stories of Castro's cruelties to the dissidents and the captured Americans. The Cubans that Castro considered traitors, were executed. Once the so-called "fair" trials started, and the American government protested maltreatment of the dissidents and Americans, the wounded received medical care and meals consisting of more than just rice. I also read how the United States pulled out during the battle and did not help the Cuban people. I was very disappointed with my new homeland's political decision and the deaths that occurred. It made me sick to my stomach.

Unfortunately, six weeks later my letter to my parents was returned and stamped, "Undeliverable." I was not surprised to discover that my letter had been opened and resealed. No other Cubans in Miami had heard from their parents either. I hoped mine were okay and not affected by the Bay of Pigs fiasco.

My final assignment was the hospital at Fort Huachuca, located in Cochise County, Arizona. The army fort, originally established on March 3, 1877 as Camp Huachuca, once housed the Buffalo Soldiers of the 10th Cavalry Regiment. The fort also now housed the United States Army Network Enterprise Technology Command (NETCOM) and the Army Intelligence Center. I was under the command of Captain Melvin Schriver, MD.

It did not take Captain Schriver long to realize that I was over-qualified for my position as an x-ray technician. Captain Schriver started assigning me additional responsibilities and directed my career path towards hospital administration. At the same time, the Captain, who also became a good friend, promoted me to the rank of sergeant.

Besides enjoying and thriving in my new army life, I met and started dating another x-ray department recruit named Judith Jones. In the summer of 1962 we were married in Bisbee, Arizona by a justice of the peace. I wished I could share the joyous news with my parents. During this time, the only news I received from my parents came in carefully-written, sanitized letters that were rare at best. It was obvious they had been opened and scrutinized. The plight of my parents was always of great concern. By contrast, my tia and I stayed in close contact, as did my maternal grandparents, who were now living in Miami.

A couple of Army friends, Craig Carpenter and Steve Mundt, and I, liked to hunt deer. In early September, we purchased hunting licenses and left the base Friday afternoon to track and shoot a white tail trophy buck. The plan was to make camp, scout for deer on Saturday, Sunday morning bag the deer, and be home in the early evening. Any later and we would be considered AWOL. We drove fifteen miles into the desert and set up a dry camp. That night we sat around the campfire and shared hunting and childhood stories. Of course, Craig and Steve were curious about my life in

Cuba. Their questions were non-stop. They were surprised by my family's wealth and prestige pre-Castro, but were more shocked by how quickly it disappeared.

At dawn, we studied our maps and plotted our strategy to locate the elusive trophy bucks. We drove another five miles deeper into the desert. To cover more ground, we split up, hiking into the desert with only our rifles, blue jeans, and t-shirts. We were totally ill- prepared.

After a few hours of hiking in the heat and finding no deer, I was thirsty and decided to turn around and return to the vehicle. Even though all the arroyos looked identical, I thought I was close to my destination. Then I looked down and realized the horrible truth—I had been walking in circles; there was more than one set of boot prints in the sand. I forced myself to sit down and try to remember any landmarks. Struggling not to panic, I thought of none. I looked at my watch and discovered it was the scheduled four p.m. rendezvous time. I believed Craig and Steve would find me, so I sat, listened intently, and waited. The silence was deafening. No one came nor did I hear any faint engine noise. The night closed in as well as the cold. Shivering, I located a few warm boulders, sat with my back leaning against them, and tried to sleep. Sunday morning, I started walking again, but this time more stiffly. Thirsty, hungry, and tired, I hiked in the direction where I thought the truck was parked. As the day progressed, so did the temperature and my thirst. Unbeknown to me, I was actually heading in the opposite direction, towards Mexico. Craig and Steve unsuccessfully scoured the area calling my name. Reluctantly, they left for the base to report me lost and organize a search party.

Sunday evening, I was very exhausted and parched. Stumbling I realized I had found a faint, narrow road in the sand. I decided that tomorrow I would follow the road, but the big question was, in which direction? With night approaching I found some warm boulders to sit against and spent another long, cold night. Looking at the stars, I knew I was AWOL. I was sure the MPs would be searching for me tomorrow, or at least I hoped they would be. I thought about my parents, my new wife, whom I knew would be very worried, a huge glass of cool water, and a big rib eye steak with all the trimmings. Finally after drifting into a restless sleep, I dreamed of my rescue and homecoming.

The next morning, with the sun climbing, I was thirsty, very thirsty, with no water in sight. I stood at the edge of the primitive road and contemplated which direction to walk. I had no idea and, with no coin to toss, I went left. I noticed I was walking much slower and starting to stumble frequently. I checked my watch; it was only a little after ten. The silence was interrupted by a faint noise. With my heart starting to pound, I stopped and listened. Is that an engine? I questioned my hearing. I even wondered if one could hear a mirage. The noise was getting louder. My heart was now pounding faster when I saw a jeep carrying two men. Using my last bit of strength, I ran toward the jeep, waving my arms and yelling. The jeep stopped and the puzzled driver, a gray-haired man, named David Johnston, wearing aviator dark glasses, looked at me. He saw a disheveled man with only a rifle, and asked, "Are you lost, son?"

I was so happy but I could only nod. David told me I better get in and come with them. As I climbed into the jeep, the passenger, Eugene Clarkston, handed me a canteen filled with cool water. Eugene then opened a lunch box and handed me an apple and some cheddar cheese. It was the best apple and cheese I had ever eaten. These two good Samaritans drove me to the base. In route I learned that if I had continued on the road, I was well on my way to Mexico. With my inherited bad sense of direction, I had, once again, picked the wrong route.

When I arrived at the base, I learned that my friends had reported me lost and the MPs were just starting to form a search party. It dawned on me that if David and Eugene had not accidentally found me, I probably would have died. I crossed myself, said a short prayer of thanks, and left to see my worried wife.

In early October 1962, Captain Schriver called me to his office. Puzzled, I stood in the doorway to be greeted and instead I was introduced to two grim army intelligence officers. They escorted me out of the hospital and drove me to a restricted, top-secret area on the 76,000-acre base. I was taken to a windowless, austere, gray room and told to sit in one of three wooden chairs placed on both sides of a grey metal table. When I tried to adjust my chair, I realized it was bolted to the floor, as was the table.

For six hours, the intelligence officers grilled me by yelling in my face, pounding the table, never smiling, and kept walking behind me and circling the table. They questioned me about my loyalty to the United States versus Cuba, my life in Cuba, why I left my homeland, and my future plans. Once they were satisfied, they drove me to the hospital. But before they let me out of the car, I was cautioned not to share our conversations; they were top secret. Still puzzled, tired, and dazed, I returned to the radiology department, where my wife, Judith, and Captain Schriver met me. They both looked worried and asked, "What was all that about?" I only shrugged and answered, "I have no idea." The agents also questioned my friends and co-workers about my loyalties. A few weeks later, it all finally made sense: the Cuban Missile Crisis had erupted. My worry and frustration about my parents intensified, but my hands were completely tied. All I could do was live my life day-by-day and I prayed for an opportunity to bring my parents to my new homeland.

Chapter Seven—Felipe and Clara—Cuban Missile Crisis

My parents settled into a burdensome routine of helping family members flee the Cuba they had once called home. In January 1962, after the United States attempted to overthrow the Castro regime with yet another failed plan named Operation Mongoose, the streets of Cienfuegos changed. By July, the military traffic grew and the heavily loaded trucks and occupants were visibly different. The soldiers were rude, loud, crowded the bars and restaurants, and spoke an unfamiliar language...Russian. The Cuban women no longer felt safe walking the streets unaccompanied by their husbands or a male family member.

With the presence of the Russians came readily available gasoline and food staples such as flour and canned goods. Unfortunately, the quality did not come close to those produced in the United States. In February, when President Kennedy imposed an embargo, shelves and bins in the markets and shops quickly became bare and food scarce. Early one morning at the butcher shop, madre was shocked to witness neighbors and acquaintances, who were actually friends, fighting over a soup bone. The winner, with a black eye and split lip, and his wife, triumphantly left the shop with their meatless bone. Shaking her head, madre knew this was only the beginning. She would be proved correct. Even after the availability of the Russian imports, the bustling black market continued to exist with farmers and backyard gardeners selling their commodities at exorbitant prices. One large papaya cost almost one week's income while a pound of beef represented the earnings from an entire month. Madre quickly realized they were lucky to have the income to afford fresh food a few times a week. However, she learned to stretch their leftovers by decreasing their portions.

The Russian agriculture and irrigation specialists' sent to save Cuba's farms and increase food production were disasters. These experts' notions of utilizing irrigation systems were dismal and laughable. The failures were not surprising, however, since the Russians' education and training were based on different climates and they stubbornly refused to learn new techniques. Thus, it was inevitable that all of their agricultural attempts failed and they were unable to resurrect the once thriving sugar cane and banana plantations. Before Castro's communist government, Cuba traded mostly with the United States and produced one-third of the world's sugar. The sugar industry, which employed over 500,000 workers, was by far the largest user of the railway system transporting the cane to mills located on the coasts. After the US embargoes, replacement markets were sought and found in other Communist countries. However, there were no competent communist workers to run and oversee the sugarcane production. The American-made equipment soon failed and parts were not available. Alternatively, the equipment from Soviet Bloc countries was inferior and took several months to arrive by sea. Due to lack of product, the new export markets soon dried up. As the Russian agriculture attempts continued to fail, my padre's friends, who had once owned the large, highly productive and profitable countryside ranches and farms, shook their heads in frustration and bewilderment. They could not understand why they, as the local experts, were not consulted. They knew it would only take two growing seasons for these tracts of land to once again become productive and profitable.

As desperation increased, food thefts became a serious problem, especially for those who owned farm animals. These animals and their by-products, eggs and milk, were now actually the property of the Communist government. The government, including the block captains, received the majority of such food, leaving only a small amount for the black market. If any animals or their by-products were stolen, the farmer was considered at fault and obligated to reimburse the government for his negligence. Most farmers could not afford to cover this government requirement. For safekeeping, at night or when the farmer was away during the day, the animals would be housed inside their tightly locked homes.

Gardens, once located in open fields or vacant lots, were now barricaded with ugly fences made from building scraps, tree debris, and junk. As the produce ripened, it would be guarded twenty-four hours a day.

Workers in hospitals and schools stole food, blankets, and medicines from the patients and students to supplement their incomes. Even though the penalty was automatically several years in prison, stealing (for many) became a way of life and survival. My parents were appalled by the daily invasive searches as they entered and left their respective places of employment. Sadly, they witnessed co-workers who, during the searches, were arrested and never seen again.

The government-controlled television broadcasts continuously bombarded Cubans with information regarding the failures of the imperialistic United States to overthrow Castro and how it would keep trying. The Soviet Union was Cuba's savior and protector. There were quotes in the Havana newspaper from Nikita Khrushchev proclaiming President Kennedy to be indecisive and weak. During this time, my parents were troubled by Kennedy's lack of backbone regarding the building of the

Berlin Wall. They were even more appalled that Kennedy had deserted the Cuban dissidents at the Bay of Pigs. Madre was awakened many times by Padre's shouting, crying, and moaning during countless nightmares. No matter how many times she asked, padre refused to tell her about the horrors he witnessed at the Bay of Pigs.

My parents became more alarmed with the arrival of 43,000 Soviet troops and missile construction crews. They were covertly comingled with agricultural specialists, but it was obvious that they were building missile sites. Even though buildings and palm trees camouflaged the missiles, the Cuban citizenry knew exactly where they were located. It was Russia and Cuba's worst kept secret. In July and August 1962, a multitude of frantic reports were forwarded to Cuban exiles living in Miami and then passed to espionage experts in the CIA. The majority of the sightings were dismissed as unbelievable or laughable, however, three reports could not be ignored by the CIA experts. The reports told of trucks hauling long cylindrical tubes covered with tarps. The tubes were so long that in some towns the trucks had problems maneuvering through the narrow streets. The loud rumbling noise and vibration of windowpanes woke many frightened people.

While the CIA thought that it could keep the extent of the Russian presence in Cuba secret, it was not the only arm of the United States that received information on the Russian involvement and its missiles. The first public notification came on August 31st when Senator Kenneth Keating shared with Congress information that had come from Cuban exiles living in Florida. He accused the Kennedy administration of covering up a major missile threat to the United States by the Soviets in Cuba. The administration and top executive and military advisors were aware of the threat, but before they could publicly confront the Russians, they needed solid evidence. Until this was in hand, the administration openly denied that Russian missiles existed in Cuba. It continued to do so even after the United States government received initial false reports from the Russian embassy declaring that the Russians had placed only a few troops in Cuba to protect their agricultural attachés. With rolling eyes and gritting teeth, the United

States government openly supported the arrival of troops to protect the "agricultural experts."

The elaborate denial and deceptions from the Soviet Union concerning its entry into Cuba to place its missiles were known as "maskirovka." Those involved, including the troops, were not aware of their missions. Some troops were even issued heavy winter clothing for maneuvers near the North Sea, only to be diverted to sunny, warm Cuba.

The Russian denials were dismissive and sometimes delivered to bewildered, or at other times, angry US officials. On September 7, 1962, the United Nations Russian Ambassador Anatoly Dobrynin told Adlai Stevenson, the United States Ambassador to the United Nations, that the Soviet Union was only supplying food and defensive weapons to Cuba. He dismissed Stevenson's questions as troublesome. He could not understand why the United States would even consider such a horrible thought! On September 11, the Soviet news agency, TASS, also denied the United States' accusations. TASS declared: the Soviets have no intention or need to have nuclear missiles in Cuba. After all, the US and Russia are friends.

However, on October 7th, there was a contradiction to the Russian propaganda. Not caring about Russia's attempted deflections, Castro ordered Cuban President Osvaldo Dorticós Torrado to deliver a strong message to the United Nations General Assembly: "If….we are attacked, we will defend ourselves. I repeat, we have sufficient means with which to defend ourselves; we have indeed our inevitable weapons, the weapons, which we would have preferred not to acquire, and which we do not wish to employ."

On October 13th, Dobrynin was again questioned, and again vehemently denied Soviet missile presence. The denials continued. On October 17th, a Soviet Senior Embassy representative delivered to Kennedy a personal message from Khrushchev to reassure Kennedy that "under no circumstances would surface-to-surface missiles be sent to Cuba." At this point, Kennedy knew better. Two days earlier, after a long wait, due mostly to hurricane weather conditions, he had received the necessary confirmation from the Air Force, which he would use shortly when he confronted the Russians.

With the heavy-handed Russian presence, my parents spent the majority of their evenings, home alone. Padre no longer met his friends at Liceo, the men's club, to sit in easy chairs on the large veranda, enjoying lively discussions, sipping French cognac, and puffing aromatic cigars. They could no longer afford the French cognac or the club's monthly dues. The new members, all Russian officers and Cuban Communist party leaders, soon overshadowed and replaced the Cubans. There were spies everywhere.

It was also the end of madre and her friends walking arm-in-arm, chatting, and laughing at each other's stories on the prado between the Avenues Santa Cruz and Santa Elena in front of our home. Their animated conversations in neighborhood coffee shops ceased, as well as visits to the yacht club.

The socioeconomic deterioration of Cuba was accompanied by the rapid decline of the arts and buildings. Once-popular performances at the 950-seat Teatro Tomas Terry, designed and built in 1888 by the family of the late Venezuelan, Tomas Terry, became a memory. Famous performers such as the French actress Sarah Bernardt, Russian Ballerina Anna Pavlova, and the Italian tenor Enrico Caruso, were just a few who had graced the stage of the once opulent theater. Money was no longer available to support such things and people stopped attending out of fear. The once proud theater soon stood silent and started its downward spiral into deterioration. My parents were saddened by the fall of this beautiful theater. They had attended all the performances and had met many of the performers.

Unbeknownst to my parents, on October 14, 1962, a United States Air Force pilot flew a Lockheed U-2 over Cuba snapping 928 photographs of the Soviet SS-4 missiles. This confirmed the missile construction sites located in western Cuba. As early as August 1962, the United States suspected the Soviets were building nine medium range missile sites. These missiles, with a 1,200-mile capability and capacity to carry thermonuclear warheads, put the southern United States within easy reach. The photographs also confirmed the existence of MIG-21 fighters and Ilyushin Il-28 light bombers scattered throughout Cuba's airfields.

A few days after confronting the Russians, and with tensions high, President Kennedy addressed his nation. He stated that while a strict quarantine of shipments heading to Cuba remained in place, only shipments carrying offensive weapons would be turned back; cargos containing necessities of life would be allowed to pass through the blockade.

Daily, Cuban newspaper and television broadcasts warned that there would be a nuclear war. Of course, it was the fault of the imperialistic United States, as Americans hated all Cubans. If the Cubans could no longer feed and clothe their families, it was due to the United States' imposed blockade. Pounding the podium with his fist, Castro shouted over and over that a blockade was an act of war. The heroes, the Soviet Union, would protect all Cubans and wipe out the imperialistic Americans. Alarmed, my parents looked at each other in disbelief. They were afraid for their relatives living in Miami.

After the first broadcast, my parents rushed to the markets. There was widespread panic and long lines. They brought home what was available. After just one day, the shelves in the stores and stalls at the markets were bare. Desperation had caused both food and civility to disappear.

After October 28th, the tone of Castro's broadcasts changed. He announced the Soviet Union had won the confrontation with the United States. The defeated imperialists would be removing their act-of-war blockade; there would soon be milk and honey for all. This time, my parents looked at each other and rolled their eyes. Obviously, Castro did not do his own shopping. He had not witnessed the shouting and fights for morsels of food and people barricading their homes in fear of thieves.

Even after the blockade ended, the market shelves never returned to normal, and the lines continued. The black market was even more active, and the lines longer, the promised milk and honey never materialized. The

Russian soldiers were always well-fed and aggressive toward the Cuban citizenry. As employment became scarcer and the applications to flee increased, Castro finally realized that the people leaving were the educated professionals. In response, he closed the border. Shoulders sagging, my parents grimly looked at each other with no hope. The brightness in their eyes continued to dim.

Chapter Eight—Felipe, Clara and Felipito

The years continued to pass slowly for both my parents. By January 1966, they had no plans and no hope of leaving Cuba. All their family members as well as many friends had fled the country. At sixty-six years of age, padre yearned to retire but the cost of living was too high. The daily drudgery made my normally vivacious madre, at forty-nine, discouraged and bitter. They shuffled through the days, weeks, and years mechanically. Unemployment levels in Cuba continued to climb. Even with the monthly coupon books issued since 1961, hunger was rampant. The thought of food was never far from a Cuban's mind. The coupons covered food, gasoline, and clothing. Madre considered them useless with the exception of gas for padre's car.

Of course, the expensive and necessary black market continued to thrive. The communist coupon stores supplied staples, rancid meats, tough bread, and old, shriveled vegetables and fruit. The dress shops for women and men faded into oblivion. The only clothing available came from Russia and was scratchy, thick, black or brown wool, or heavy cotton. Stylish shoes no longer existed. Instead, they were clunky, and were only available in two colors, ugly black or brown. The thick, droopy cotton stockings were a hideous beige. Sheer nylon stockings were a coveted luxury; even on the black market, they were hard to get and very expensive. Madre spent numerous evenings patching and darning clothes, and very carefully tatting her nylon stockings.

As a girl, madre had learned to sew on her mother's Singer treadle machine. Now she wished she still had it. Her mother and father had sold or given away all their belongings when they left Cuba. Madre sighed, "What can I do?" One morning while seeing a frail psychotherapy patient, she had an idea. Her face broke into a smile as she snapped her fingers, making her neurotic patient jump. Her solution required dealing on the black market. Madre shook her head and closed her eyes; she had to be very cautious. People who flashed money had a tendency to disappear, so she planned to approach only trustworthy vendors.

At home during lunch which consisted of one egg cooked with leftover peppers and onions, accompanied by small portions of rice and a fried plantain, she discussed her idea with padre. After he told her to be very careful, Padre agreed it would be worth the expense and the risk. He knew she needed a challenge and something to keep her busy. Staying home in the evenings and weekends was very difficult for her; she was very restless. After lunch she washed and dried the dishes. She then saved the oil from frying the plantains and put it in the refrigerator since frying oils and lard were both very difficult to find and expensive, even on the black market.

After work she hurried by taxi to the market and, in hushed tones, spoke to Julio, who sold vegetables. He blinked and quickly whispered, "No," but added loudly, "I have more tomatoes and onions coming Saturday."

Saturday arrived and my parents walked to the market. For fifteen minutes they waited in line when madre finally made eye contact with Julio. He smiled and said, "Buenos dias, Clara. I have your special order of tomatoes, onions, and garlic. You will have a grand party as I included all the trimmings to make your order special." Madre, trying hard to contain her excitement, returned his smile and answered, "Julio, I hope I can afford all the trimmings."

"What about the cost of the vegetables and a pair of beautiful nylon stockings. I want my wife's legs to be as shapely and fine as yours," Julio said, followed by a nod and a wink.

Gritting his teeth, padre started to interject, but madre put her hand on his arm and stepped forward. She understood they had no negotiating power and asked, "Can you deliver the vegetables this evening? The order is much too heavy for us to carry."

"Of course. See you at seven."

Julio delivered a Singer treadle machine in perfect working order. Madre was ecstatic. She immediately made plans to design patterns and sew blouses using fabric from her evening gowns. As she touched the beautiful gowns, she was flooded with fond memories and was overcome by emotion. She sat down and, with her head in her hands, sobbed. Her life would never be the same.

Finally, after several weeks of frustrating trial and error, madre modeled her first blouse and skirt for padre. Padre was astonished, "Clara, I had no idea you were so talented! But where on earth did you get the fabric?" As she explained, he shook his head in awe. It was not long before padre had a new suit and shirt made from his tuxedos. Madre was grateful to have a new activity to keep her mind busy.

During a hot August day before lunch, padre walked briskly into the house shaking a letter and shouting, "Clara, Clara, I have wonderful news!" Madre, washing dishes, dried her hands, pulled the letter from padre's hands, and quickly read it. "My God, Felipe," she enthused, "This is our ticket out!"

The letter was an invitation from the University of Mexico Medical School, and included a plane ticket. Padre had been invited to speak at an international medical symposium in June 1967. Obviously, the letter had been opened and read. It was stamped with "Approved" and the date. It was unbelievable. They would be able to leave after all! His excitement and happiness were infectious. Madre was so happy but then she thought, "Felipe, does this include me?"

Padre stopped and stammered, "Clara, I am not sure. Let me make a phone call." He called the Cienfuegos Communist Headquarters and was told no, it was only approved for him. Couples were not allowed to travel together. Deflated, he hugged her. With tears, she stepped back and bravely told him, "Felipe, go. Get out of Cuba! This mess is killing you. You and Felipito will figure out a way for me to leave too. I will be okay."

For days padre watched as my madre tried to hide her emotions. She bounced from elation to anger and then resentment. Padre was torn. He loved this woman but was overwhelmed by thoughts of escape and, ultimately, freedom. He was also terrified of what the future could hold. Then he had an idea and said a prayer asking for what he knew would be a miracle. Father carefully penned an acceptance letter to Carlos Mendez at the University of Mexico to speak at the symposium. He also suggested that Dr. Mendez consider inviting Clara Hidalgo de Posada to present her co-authored paper on the psychological effects of surgical procedures. After much consideration, he decided not to share his plan with my madre. He could not bear telling her in case his plan failed. He also wrote a letter to a friend who had opted to reside in Mexico City instead of the United States. He shared that he was coming to Mexico City to speak at a medical symposium. He asked if the friend would notify other acquaintances of his arrival so they could perhaps have dinner.

A month later, now living in central Washington State, I opened a letter with a return address of Mexico City from Eduardo Ochoa, an old friend of my father. I read the letter and was surprised by its contents. With my heart pounding, I reread it two more times and each time was more dumbstruck. I questioned what I was actually seeing. After Castro closed the border, I had given up hope of my parents ever leaving Cuba.

Then I realized the horrible truth. Only my padre was arriving in Mexico. I telephoned Mirtila long distance in Miami. She was just as surprised and knew nothing more. After talking another five minutes, I told her I would keep her informed. I hung up and quickly answered the letter. I would definitely come to Mexico and then I inquired about my madre. Was she still alive? I did not want to ask but knew I needed to know why she was not accompanying my father.

After I was honorably discharged from the US Army in 1963, I received several job offers. After visiting the Seattle 1962 World's Fair during July with Army buddy Robert Johnson, I fell in love with the Pacific Northwest. Robert and his parents introduced me to the scenic Cascade and Olympic Mountain ranges and Mount Rainier Park. I was awed. I had never seen such majestic and rugged mountains and beautiful forests. I knew in my heart this was the area where I wanted to settle, so I accepted employment as the Radiology Chief at a Catholic Hospital in Yakima, Washington. In 1963, Judith and I made the move from southern Arizona to Washington.

I was delighted to embrace the area's activities and became an avid outdoorsman. I fly fished, hunted, white water rafted, hiked, camped, and even learned to snow ski. I was always busy. Now all this had to be placed on the back burner until I brought my father to the United States. Hopefully, if my madre was still alive she would come too.

Six weeks later, I received an answer from Eduardo Ochoa in Mexico. My madre appeared to be well but Castro would not allow couples to travel together. My padre planned to attend the symposium alone. I was relieved about my madre, but was saddened that she was stuck in Cuba. I made reservations to fly to Mexico City in June, but I had a puzzle to solve. How could I bring my padre to the United States from Mexico?

Padre also received a letter from Eduardo Ochoa inquiring about my madre's health; he replied the same day. His guilt was monumental. One day he was going to Mexico, and the next he was going to stay in Cuba. The uncertainty was taking a toll on his relationship with my madre. Madre continued to be brave but her resentment was difficult to conceal. Their dinner conversations were shallow and only civility remained.

The Christmas season passed uneventfully and no gifts were exchanged. My padre thought, "What happened to our joy?" He noticed madre had altered all their clothes. They were both losing weight as food was increasingly difficult to find and very expensive. He was always amazed by how she managed to put food on the table at all. One morning they were eating breakfast consisting of café con leche, dry toast (the only way to eat the Russian bread), and one poached egg, when there was a loud pounding on their front door. Padre opened the door to find Block Captain Jorge Elizondo and two soldiers. Captain Elizondo informed him, "We are here to escort Clara Hidalgo de Posada to headquarters."

Puzzled, my padre answered, "Jorge, what does headquarters want with my wife?"

"It is not your concern. This only involves Clara," he retorted.

Madre immediately turned white and felt ill. Swallowing hard, she calmly fetched her purse and joined Captain Elizondo. On their way out the door, she turned to padre, attempted to speak but failed, instead she smiled, and patted his arm. She was put in the back seat of a boxy, black, Russian Lada and driven to Communist headquarters. She was placed in an austere room with only a wooden table and two hard wooden chairs. There was no window. Madre sat with her purse in her lap and crossed her legs. She refused to be intimidated and called upon her training as a psychologist. She forced her mind wander back to pleasant memories.

After making her wait for more than an hour, the door abruptly opened. A tall, blond Russian officer, whom she did not recognize, quickly walked into the room and calmly sat on the other chair. "Let me introduce myself, Clara Hildago de Posada, I am Colonel Petrov." My madre nodded and looked him in the eyes. Colonel Petrov, looking back at her, continued, "Let me ask you about your co-authored paper about the psychological effects patients experience after surgery."

Madre frowned and asked, "Why do you need this information?" He narrowed his eyes and retorted, "I do not need a reason. I am your superior. Therefore, you will answer my questions."

Madre not wanting to make him angry; quickly smiled and answered, "As you wish, Colonel Petrov."

Colonel Petrov replied, "Good, now that you understand, my first question is: What is the major problem people experience?"

Madre, still puzzled about why she was there, put on her doctor persona and answered, "Patients experience a number of trauma-related issues that can be attributed to anesthesia. The most common are endocrine and metabolic. These post surgery complications are different for men and women, depending on the type, length, seriousness of the surgery, and the part of the body involved."

Petrov, attempting to look as if he understood, murmured, "What do you mean by endocrine and metabolic?"

Madre looked directly at him and answered innocently, "Do you want the long answer, which could take days, or the abbreviated version?"

"Let's start with the abbreviated version and if I need additional information, I will ask you. However, I want to warn you there is an experienced doctor who is intently listening to this conversation so do not try to impress or lie to me," Petrov sneered.

In earnest, madre explained, taking a full hour. When she finished, Colonel Petrov left the room and returned thirty minutes later. He had a sheet of paper containing numerous handwritten questions. The list of questions, madre assumed, had been written by the hidden doctor. She realized she had to be very careful with her answers, as the doctor probably had read her paper.

For the rest of the day, she answered Petrov's questions succinctly. She had no idea of the time, but she knew it was late and she was exhausted. Colonel Petrov again left the room. She refused to cry or look scared, and was determined to continue her professional persona, but her heart was beating rapidly. She knew the discussion in the other room was about her. She closed her eyes and said a silent, quick prayer, "Please God, make my death quick." As she opened her eyes, Colonel Petrov strode into the room. He came to her side of the table, shook her hand, declared, "The Cuban government and its Russian partners are very proud to have one of its women as accomplished and poised as you, Comrade Clara Hidalgo de

Posada. We are delighted that in June you will be presenting your paper at the International Medical Symposium in Mexico City. You are a hero and mentor to all Cuban and Russian women."

Bewildered, madre exclaimed, "Colonel Petrov, thank you for your kind words. I do not know what you are talking about!"

Petrov answered, "Dr. Hidalgo de Posada, you will when you arrive home and read this file. Since your husband will remain in Cuba, I will personally escort you to the Havana airport. I do not want such a dignified woman as you traveling alone."

Madre stammered, "I do not want to impose on you, Colonel." He raised his head, looked at her, and replied, "Nonsense, I would be delighted. I will see you in June. My secretary will make the arrangements." Then he briskly left her standing dumbfounded.

She hurried out of the interrogation room and found the bored Block Captain waiting. He escorted her to the car and drove her home. She controlled her elation and maintained a dignified silence. She did not dare open the file knowing that Captain Elizondo was watching her.

The normal fifteen-minute drive seemed to take forever but they finally arrived home. The word "home" suddenly took on a different meaning. She knew it was now only a temporary sanctuary. Knowing that Captain Elizondo was still watching, she willed herself to walk slowly up the steps to the portico. She opened the door to my worried padre, closed it quickly, and led him to the dining room. Smiling, she silently studied the file's contents and handed them to padre. He opened it and looked at her in utter surprise. She finally let the tears flow and his eyes also filled. This was the second time in her marriage that she experienced seeing him with tears. "Clara, you are going to Mexico City too!" my padre exclaimed. She gleefully nodded and dabbed her eyes. He added, "I am so pleased!" She smiled and nodded once again.

It was close to nine p.m. and suddenly they were both famished and emotionally drained. First, madre wanted to take a shower to erase the smell of the Communist headquarters and Captain Elizondo's car. She then prepared a simple meal of a Spanish tortilla and fried plantains. Over dinner they discussed their June departure plans. They knew they dared not be seen traveling together nor could they tell anyone about their plans. The next five months would pass quickly and there was much to do.

My padre also explained, "Clara, you need to send a very carefully worded letter to Señor Ochoa and ask him to invite your friends to have dinner when you arrive. I am sure he will write to Felipito." Early the next morning, my parents penned the letter together and mailed it on their way to work. They also mailed her letter of acceptance to speak at the symposium.
In March, I opened another letter from Señor Ochoa. I read the letter two times. I jumped out of my chair and whooped and hollered "Yeah!" I had no idea how my madre did it, but she was speaking at the symposium too! I was sure I would hear some very interesting stories. June 16th could not arrive fast enough.

My parents went about their work and home life as if nothing had changed. They told no one about the medical symposium and especially their attendance. Madre decided to alter one of padre's suits for him and make a new suit for herself using her wedding dress and one of his summer suits. As she cut the beautiful ivory satin fabric for her blouse, she reminisced about her wedding. The more than thirty years had quickly passed and she had no idea what the new future would hold for the two of them. She only hoped my padre, who was very set in his ways, could adapt. Padre's navy, summer-weight suit material and color perfectly complemented her blouse. It was a classic combination. As she altered my padre's suit and sewed her skirt and jacket, she added paper currency to serve as the interfacing. Her suit jacket sleeve edges contained rings that left no lumps or indentations. She pried the backs from her earrings, used the fronts as buttons, and intertwined the colors so they matched decoratively. Her bracelets and necklaces were placed in the hems of Felipe's pants and sleeves. She was hoping if they were frisked, their arms, legs, skirt and pants hems would not be touched. She deftly removed all the precious gems from her remaining jewelry and my padre's cufflinks. She also put jewels and money in the clothing she planned to pack. When she finished, she crossed herself and said a prayer. Without the jewels and money, they would have nothing when they arrived in Mexico or the United States.

She also hid family photographs and negatives in her clothing, purse, and suitcase lining. She wanted the new generation to have the photographs so they could learn of their proud heritage. She looked forward to meeting my new son, Phillip. My madre knew her daughter, Mirtila, had two children in Cuba before they left and she looked forward to seeing both her children and grandchildren. Her arms ached to give them all hugs. As June 16th approached, their anticipation and nervousness grew.

Madre walked several times through her beautiful home, touching, and fondly bidding farewell to many works of art, furniture, and knickknacks. She was especially sad to leave her treadle Singer sewing machine. It was like leaving an old friend. She knew that once it was discovered that my parents were not returning, the house would be ransacked and several families would be assigned to live in the house. It always happened. Many times she would see friends' items for sale on the black market. Hers would soon be there, too. They visited their remaining Cuban friends. They could not say goodbye, but they could at least give them one last handshake or hug. They wished they could be honest and give them their possessions.

The big day finally arrived! Even though madre knew her suitcase would be inspected, she packed all her favorite clothes and shoes in it. It was heavy. She sighed and hoped Colonel Petrov's clout would get her bag through customs untouched. Right on time, Colonel Petrov arrived to pick her up. Padre escorted her to the car, gave her a hug, a kiss goodbye, smiled and said, "Clara, I will see you in two weeks." After madre left, my padre impatiently pacing, waited fifteen minutes and then followed in his car.

My parents had decided once they both arrived at the Havana airport, they would neither acknowledge one another nor sit together. Hoping this ruse would work, they also planned not to sit together on the plane. They would not feel safe until they cleared customs in Mexico City.

Cuba and Beyond...The Journey

My madre's ride with Colonel Petrov was a long and boring one with him expounding in broken Spanish about his career, his homeland, blah, blah, and blah, blah. She spent the time smiling, nodding, and complimenting him. He exceeded her hopes at the airport. He continued pushing his authority by checking her in for the flight, shoving the suitcase through and declaring, "An inspection is not necessary, this woman is a hero!" As he left madre at the gate, he declared he would meet her plane in two weeks and kissed her hand. As Colonel Petrov finally bid her farewell, madre saw a tense padre enter the waiting room. She walked away and stared out the window seeing nothing but his reflection in the glass as he took a seat with his back to her.

Again thanks to Colonel Petrov, she boarded the Aeronaves de Mexico Douglas DC-6 first. When padre walked past her, she was looking out the window saying her last goodbye to her homeland. She had her speech in her lap and planned to study it during the flight. She needed the diversion to keep from crying. As she glanced at the people boarding, she wondered if they were escaping or leaving on business. She figured they probably had the same thoughts. As the plane taxied, she started to breathe a little easier.

The three-hour flight seemed like an eternity. When the plane finally touched down in Mexico City, madre started holding her breath. She would be very nervous until her visa and passport were both stamped. As the plane stopped and the door opened, she said another prayer. She knew she was not the only one praying. She put on her sunglasses, walked down the stairs, and breathed in the air. It smelled like freedom. She shook her head and forced herself to face reality. With only one step remaining, she could not keep from feeling euphoric despite having no country to call home.

My padre watched as madre walked down the stairs with dignity, crossed the tarmac, and entered the terminal. He was profoundly relieved that they were escaping together. But he wondered, escaping to what? They had only a tourist visa and would soon be required to return to Cuba. He sure hoped I had a plan.

Diana Posada

After clearing customs, my jubilant parents carried their suitcases into the terminal's main waiting area and smiled at the large banner hanging from the ceiling, "Welcome to Mexico!" When she saw me, my madre suddenly dropped her suitcase and began to sob as she ran to me and threw her arms around me. My padre, now carrying two suitcases, joined us. We all hugged and shook hands and then hugged Eduardo Ochoa. Within thirty minutes we were in Eduardo's car and on our way to his ranch. The conversations were lively and animated. All our faces shined with love while we continually touched each other. My parents had made it to Mexico. They had no idea what their futures held, but right now they did not care.

Chapter Nine—Felipe, Clara and Felipito—Mexico

S taying with the Ochoas at their country home fifteen miles outside of Mexico City, there were many discussions about Castro, Cuba's disintegration, and the plight of my parents. I was very disheartened to hear about my padre's conscripted role at the Bay of Pigs, the maltreatment of the dissidents, and the Russians' involvement with Castro and the Cuban missile crisis. I noticed my parents had lost weight - over twenty pounds each. They explained the average monthly wage in Cuba had sunk to the equivalent of twenty to thirty US dollars. As medical professionals, my parents had each earned fifty dollars per month. I wondered out loud how they were able to help our relatives or as Castro called them gusanos (worms) so generously during their struggle to depart Cuba.

Madre quickly answered, "Soup and more soup."

Diana Posada

No wonder the Cuban people as a nation had each lost an average of twenty pounds. Finding food was now at the forefront of everyone's mind. My madre had many stories about the infamous black market and government stores. Some were funny but most were tragic about the fights for meat and having to stand under the hot sun for hours in long lines.

Sadly, madre declared, "Castro will never lose power. He is indoctrinating the children at school in all grade levels in the communist way of life. You should read the new Marxist textbooks. These children have lost the ability to think independently. Felipito, this started near the time you left. Many are now in their teens and the brightest are pre-ordained for career paths in the communist party."

Nodding, padre added, "Remember how Castro denounced Batista over and over again as a horrible dictator and a cowardly man?" Everyone nodded. He continued, "Castro immediately took control by placing his cronies in high-level government and civilian jobs. Many who originally held these positions, were denounced and disappeared. Castro's puppets are the only Cubans making a decent living."

Shaking my head many times during the stories, I understood the desperation to flee the homeland. It was unbelievable that a country that was once considered a paradise was now a deteriorating mess! I was relieved I had left but still felt guilty that I had deserted my parents. In unison, we all sighed and realized that under Castro's communist regime our homeland had turned its back on its own people. Quickly, the conversations changed and were directed toward future plans with renewed hope.

When my parents attended and gave their presentations at the International Medical Symposium, they had a wonderful time freely interacting with their peers from all over the world. They visited specifically with professors and doctors from the United States, Mexico, and Spain, gathering information about practicing in their respective countries. They both concluded it would be much easier to immigrate to Spain or stay in Mexico.

Cuba and Beyond...The Journey

My parents hoped to settle in the United States, but obtaining a permanent resident status would be difficult. Their English, especially padre's, was not very good. Madre had a better grasp because her parents had sent her to English classes in the United States. She could proficiently read and write in English and I knew it would only take practice to improve her speaking skills. Padre could read English but spoke slowly with a heavy accent. Madre believed that once my padre was forced to speak English, he would easily pick it up. She worried about him being able to transfer his medical license, however. He would definitely need to learn how to write using more sophisticated English. In Cuba, my parents had wanted to improve their language skills, but they never dared for fear of being jailed, or worse. They never truly felt safe even in their own home. Friends had whispered to be very careful, as they had witnessed neighborhood captains standing at doors and windows looking and listening.

I remained in Mexico another week while my parents shared more stories about the hardships of the "new" Cuba. I could clearly see they were elated to be in Mexico, but I was alarmed as I examined their faces. What concerned me was their eyes. The eyes, often described as the windows to one's soul, were certainly revealing for my parents. Their eyes no longer sparkled but, instead, now mirrored sadness even when they laughed. I hoped once they were settled, this sadness would disappear.

I also realized that it landed squarely on my shoulders to find a way for my parents to enter the United States. Indeed, I had a heavy burden. The research I performed before I traveled to Mexico indicated that the immigration process was convoluted and could take years. Getting my parents into the United States would definitely become my full time job until they gained entry. The only saving grace was Plan B; they could stay in Mexico or immigrate to Spain. However, I did not want this, even though my parents downplayed Plan B as not a problem. Secretly, I knew it was. My parents wanted to live in Miami close to their family and friends. I knew they would definitely need the help of their family and friends to quickly settle into a new way of life. The Miami area already had many Cuban businesses that catered to the growing numbers of Cubans and Latin Americans immigrating to the area. The climate where I lived in Washington would be much too cold for them and they would have no friends, American or Cuban.

We called Marta and asked for her advice. Marta informed my parents, "Stay in Mexico until you can obtain your permanent resident status. Do not enter the United States without it. If you do, you will have to leave and then reapply."

Eduardo also reminded my parents that their visitor's visas were expiring in another week. Bewildered, they looked at each other as Eduardo continued, "You can live here as long as you need and use this address as your place of residence. Felipito and I will go tomorrow and investigate the Mexican visitor visa process." We all nodded in agreement.

Eduardo added, "I do not want the Mexican authorities to know your location just in case the Cuban government contacts them. I do not think you are in danger, but I think we should keep who is seeking residency quiet until we know the process."

My madre shivered as she thought of Colonel Petrov's anger when he discovered she would not be returning to Cuba. She knew he would take special delight in personally pulling the trigger at her execution.

The next morning, Eduardo and I drove to Mexico City. Eduardo indicated that today they would investigate whose palms they needed to grease and just how greedy those palms were. Many times during their meetings we wanted to reach across the desk and choke the smiling, sarcastic clerk. The day was long, hot, and frustrating, but we successfully accomplished our mission.

After several hundred dollars of greasing several palms, my parents were granted the necessary visitor visas to stay in Mexico. They were not allowed to work but at least they were safe. I left relieved they had somewhere to live.

After I returned to central Washington, I continued working through the complicated immigration procedure. Over and over, I read the Cuban

Adjustment Act trying to find anything that would help. The law was enacted by Congress and signed by President Lyndon Johnson on November 2, 1966. However, since my parents landed in Mexico and not the United States, I was told the law did not apply. Frustrated and stymied for over a month, I was no closer to answering the questions "how and what" than when I had started.

One evening after experiencing another long, frustrating day, I was meeting with the head radiologist, Dr. John Turner, when he asked how my parents liked the United States. Tired, I snorted and replied, "They are stuck in Mexico." I explained the dilemma and what I had been told by the immigration experts and attorneys. Dr. Turner instructed me to sit tight and let him make a few phone calls. Puzzled, I thanked him and nodded in agreement. I really had no other choice.

Working in my office two weeks later, I received a phone call from Lucy, an aide of Catherine May, a member of the United Stated Congress. Representative May was born and raised in central Washington and was the first woman elected to hold office in the state. Lucy told me the congresswoman felt the plight of my family deeply, and therefore would assist in facilitating and expediting the documentation process for permanent resident status. I immediately mailed the requested documentation directly to Lucy. The congresswoman kept her promise and, within a month, the permanent resident status cards arrived by a courier service. Elated, I quickly made arrangements to fly to Mexico City.

Two weeks later, the three Posadas landed in central Washington. My parents were delighted to meet their daughter-in-law, Judith, and new grandson, also named Felipe. Judith and I served as tour guides introducing them to the beauty of Mount Rainier, Paradise Lodge, Seattle, Mount Adams, and many other majestic sights. My parents understood why I loved the rugged Northwest but expressed their desire for me and my family to move to Miami. I smiled and shook my head---an emphatic no.

After another two weeks and several telephone conversations later with Juan Jose, Mirtila, and Marta, my parents were eager to start their new lives in Miami. They planned to live with madre's parents until they located jobs. Everyone understood it could take up to a year to obtain the necessary paperwork and licenses to practice in their respective fields.

As they walked from the Miami airport to the arms of waiting family members, my parents stopped, looked at each other, hugged and smiled. It was hard to believe that after seven long years, they had finally escaped Castro's brutal repression and gained their long lost freedom.

Epilogue

My parents quickly discovered that life in Miami was totally different than Cuba, before and after Castro. The days of walking to the markets, friends' homes, and restaurants no longer existed. Urban sprawl dictated the necessity of a car. My madre, who had never driven, had no choice but to learn to drive. After many arguments and tears, her first driver education teacher, my impatient padre, threw his hands up in the air and gave up. Fortunately, madre's father, Juan Jose, possessed the necessary tolerance, and soon she proudly earned her first driver's license. After madre gained her freedom, the sky was the limit!

Many crazy stories arose out of her automobile antics. For example, while driving to shopping malls and luncheons with friends and family, she was unable to keep both hands on the wheel and not use them to dramatize her conversations. Other passengers, wide-eyed from their adventures with her, shared that madre would actually stop in her lane of traffic to finish a conversation while ignoring the honking horns and shaking fists of disgusted, passing motorists. Even if the ride was only a block long, friends and family always raced to sit in the back seat.

After studying a city map, madre drove to Miami University to transfer her credentials in order to work. This process was greatly accelerated due to the fact she had hidden her diplomas and certifications in her suitcase lining. Madre had so carefully stitched and glued her papers into the lining that it was invisible to the naked eye, and, thanks to Colonel Petrov, her suitcase was never examined or even opened. Alas, the process to obtain her American doctorate appeared to be too lengthy and time-consuming. After discussing her options with a university counselor, she decided instead to acquire a master's degree in order to teach.

Miami University then offered madre a teaching position and she started to work almost immediately. With the large influx of Cubans, and Central and South Americans, she taught English as a second language to classrooms full of eager students. Part of her class curriculum was to require the students, who were a minimum of eighteen years old, to describe in their native Spanish language, where they grew up, and how and why they immigrated to the United States. This exercise greatly assisted in her understanding of each student's motivation and ability to learn a second language. She also learned of each student and their family's plight, and the difficulties they now faced in the United States as new immigrants. She realized how lucky she was that her father had had the foresight to anticipate the needs for each family member's assimilation. Her heart went out to many whom she tried to help. During the first few weeks, madre discovered she enjoyed teaching and did not miss treating patients. Moreover, thanks to her income and ability to save, my parents were able to plan a timeline for the purchase of their own home. It seemed strange to them at their ages to be living with parents.

Madre and her mother hosted dinner and card parties for friends and family from Cuba. These two outgoing women both quickly acclimated to their new lives. They thoroughly enjoyed renewing old friendships and starting new ones. After seven years of not entertaining and experiencing food and clothing shortages, madre was astounded at the large shopping malls and grocery stores. At first, it was shocking to find everything she required to cook a meal under one roof. For months, she shook her head in awe at the shelves stuffed with canned foods, coolers with fresh produce, large cold cases filled with meat and seafood, and freezers filled with ice and ice cream. She was delighted! The shopping malls provided even more hours of entertainment. She never tired of touching and trying on new, modern clothing. She always smiled when she entered a shoe department. The shoes from Spain, France, and Italy were attractively arranged in every color and style. Not one clunky, ugly Russian shoe was anywhere to be seen. She did not miss the black market with people pushing and yelling, but she had to admit that she missed the price haggling.

My padre's adaptation was difficult. To practice medicine, he had to pass the US medical boards. At sixty-seven years of age, this was not an easy task. It had been over forty years since he had passed his Cuban medical boards. Even though he was advised against it, he decided to take the written boards. Unfortunately, he did not succeed. He was exasperated, perplexed, and had a huge dilemma: he needed to work, but in order to practice medicine he was required to pass the medical boards. He now understood that in order to pass he had to study and study hard. Living in a very noisy Cuban household that offered neither peace and quiet nor a place to study, he felt like a dog chasing its tail. He was very frustrated and cranky.

To practice English, he read the Miami Herald newspaper daily. The Herald established in September 1903, carried stories of Latin America, and, of course, Cuba. Padre noticed that each day he read the paper, his reading pace and comprehension improved. One day a solution to his problem appeared in the newspaper. He smiled when he found a large display ad from a cruise company. The company sailing out of Miami was advertising for a doctor; international medical credentials were acceptable. The only complication was that he was required to sign a two-year contract. After a quick discussion, my parents decided he should apply to determine if his Cuban medical credentials were acceptable. Madre did not look forward to his long absences, but she knew he needed to work. My padre had become angry, agitated, and withdrawn.

Padre learned during his interview that the company would indeed accept his credentials and he would definitely have time to study for the US medical boards. He was hired as the ship's medical officer and was required to be at sea forty-eight weeks each year. Madre was allowed to visit two weeks every year. After two years of working and studying long hours, padre passed his written and oral medical boards. He had enjoyed his status as the ship's medical officer but liked having his feet on dry land more.

With Juan Jose's financial help, padre opened a small medical practice treating many of his patients from Cuba as well as their American friends and relatives. He was very happy to be working and able to visit with old and new patients daily. His hospital privileges permitted him to attend to his more seriously ill patients. However, the hospital was large and he was continuously getting lost. Fortunately, once the nursing staff realized his directional challenges, one of nurses would always accompany him during his rounds. For padre, walking the halls of a hospital, smelling the antiseptic, and listening to the organized chaos, was home. He was the happiest when at the hospital and his office.

After a year, my parents managed to purchase a home close to her place of employment. In addition, since madre did the majority of the shopping and padre was always at work, they purchased a second car. Madre helped my reluctant padre pass the Florida written and driving tests. Fortunately, due to his lack of directional sense, he traveled only back and forth to work. He always carried a map, with his routes to the hospital and his office clearly outlined in red. If he drove to other destinations, he would always have a passenger who provided explicit directions.

Padre was shocked at the daily pace. He felt there was no time to just relax and sip a scotch. If my parents, who enjoyed being social, were not at home, they were visiting either relatives or friends. Even though padre appeared to be enjoying his new freedoms, he was never totally content. His heart still yearned for his pre-Castro Cuba. He knew this would never happen but he still missed his home and country. When at the age of seventy-seven he became ill with gall bladder disease, he opted not to have surgery. I tried to talk him into the life-saving surgery but my padre shook his head no, and within a few months he passed away dreaming of his homeland.

Madre sold their home and purchased a one-bedroom condo in a gated community. She continued teaching and hosting bridge parties until her mid-seventies. She frequently attended concerts and visited art galleries. Even though she could now afford to buy new clothes, she purchased a state-of-the art sewing machine and continued to design and make her own creations. She always had great satisfaction picking out new shoes to match her garments. Throughout the years, she and her friends traveled the world either on tours or cruises. When home, she babysat her great grandchildren and told them stories about the "old" Cuba. Even though she lived an additional twenty-four years after padre, my madre never remarried or met another permanent companion.

Unfortunately, my madre's prediction about the fate of our Cuban home, "Casa de Los Leones," proved correct. In the late 1990s, Mirtila, her daughter, visited Cienfuegos and the family residence. Mirtila sobbed as she related the devastation that had befallen it. The once proud bronze lions were scratched and dented. It appeared that people had beaten them with metal objects and scratched in their initials with sharp objects. The home's interior, filled with a shoe repair shop together with ten families who now called it home, was filthy, smelly, and in ruins. The courtyard was full of trash and the trees were dead. The interior marble slabs located on the floors and walls had been removed, and the ceilings, scarred by many years of water damage, were propped up with large tree branches and other debris. Everything of value that could be carried away and sold had been stripped from the once ornate British Embassy that later had become the Hidalgo/Posada residence. Sadly, this was not the only building or home that had been ruined. All buildings and residences in Cuba were dilapidated

Diana Posada

with the exception of the homes of the Communist elite and the government buildings. Cuba had descended to the condition of a third world country.

Then in 1981, the Urban Historic Centre of Cienfuegos became one of nine locations in Cuba to be recognized by the United Nations Educational, Scientific and Cultural Organization (UNESCO) as a World Heritage Site. UNESCO was impressed by Cienfuegos's neoclassic and eclectic styles, where the combination is unique and harmonious. The downtown area, the only place in the Caribbean with such a large cluster of neoclassical buildings, has a total of over 1,500 structures. The construction started in 1819 with the first six structures, 300 more from 1851 to 1900, and the final 1,200 being added in the 20th century. UNESCO also appreciated that Cienfuegos was actually the first city in Latin America to reflect the Spanish Enlightenment Implementation, which had been dedicated to modernity, hygiene, and urban planning. The city center was laid out in a geometric grid with ample public places for people to meet and enjoy various functions. UNESCO named a cathedral, ceremonial arch, botanical garden, fortress, park, Arch of Triumph, Teatro Tomas Terry, the University of Cienfuegos, and two cemeteries as historical sites. The Reina Cemetery is one of these sites and is where the Posada and Hidalgo families both have pantheons.

More recently, the lions located in front of our former home, La Casa de Los Leones, were repaired. Unfortunately, the interior of the home was not touched and is still in disrepair. The yacht club, co-founded by my grandfather, Juan Jose, where my parents met and spent many fun filled days with other family members and friends sitting by the pool, sampling exotic drinks in the bar, and eating delicious food prepared by the French chef Mr. Mür, is now a state-run restaurant that serves mediocre Cuban food called Club Cienfuegos.

Since UNESCO has taken such an interest in Cuba and especially Cienfuegos, the number of visiting tourists who seek to experience the history of this special city has greatly increased. While there are hotels, restaurants, and many activities available for the tourists, these attractions remain out of financial reach for the normal Cuban citizens who are still struggling to survive on twenty to thirty dollars per month.

Even though their hearts and dreams are still in Cuba, the Posada family and millions of Cuban immigrants quickly adjusted to their new American homeland and gratefully embraced all its freedoms. However, this first generation of immigrants has never forgotten the plight of the men and women who were and are still trapped in Cuba and, on a daily basis, face hunger, the repressions of Castro and his henchmen, and the deprivations caused by communism. These Cubans hold out hope that the second, third, and future generations of Cuban Americans will remember the stories they heard from their parents and grandparents about the old Cuba and why they fled their beloved homeland. They also pray that these younger generations will never forget the plight of those still suffering in Cuba.

Diana Posada

About The Author

Diana Posada, the author, is married to Felipito and feels privileged and excited to share his family's plight and escape from Cuba in Cuba and Beyond...The Journey. While this is her first book, she has started writing a sequel. Now that she is retired, Diana has more time for research and is looking forward to writing additional books.

When not writing, Diana and Felipito enjoy traveling, fly-fishing, hunting and spending time with friends. They especially enjoy having lively dinner conversations inspired by a good bottle of wine.

To contact the author: goddessposada@gmail.com

Diana Posada

Made in the USA
Middletown, DE
15 November 2018